Blake dived back in for another taste, leaving Madison breathless and gasping.

As his mouth traveled from her lips, over her jaw, to her neck, she struggled to pull air into her lungs. The excitement of his touch, the racing of her pulse, the need to press herself closer to him despite the heat in the air... How was this happening?

Madison rocked forward. Blake gasped against her skin, his hands squeezing around her arms. "Madison," he groaned.

One last hot, openmouthed kiss against the pounding at the base of her throat, then he pulled back. "We have to stop. Right now."

"Why?" she whispered. She should know the answer, but right now it was as far from her as possible.

"We have to," he said. He rested his forehead against her collarbone, breathing heavily in the hush of the garden. "I had no idea how addictive you would be."

* * *

Reclaiming His Legacy by Dani Wade
is part of the Louisiana Legacies series.

Dear Reader,

I didn't realize when I set out to write my Louisiana Legacies series how prominent the ideas of abuse and neglect of women would be. Some of those themes blossomed from my own life experiences, and some of them from the lives of women and children around me.

My hope is that while this is the backdrop of the book, it isn't the focus. More important is the willingness of others to see this plight and do something about it. While Blake finds himself in the untenable position of having to deceive Madison, he's doing it for the best of reasons: to save his stepsister from the same neglected, damaged childhood he himself endured. Madison herself has a servant's heart, willing to go above and beyond in her love for others. This leaves their hearts vulnerable but also leads them to a love like no other.

May we all have hearts that love just as deeply and care about the plights of those around us.

I love to hear from my readers! You can email me at readdaniwade@gmail.com or follow me on Facebook. As always, news about my releases is easiest to find through my author newsletter, which you can sign up for from my website at daniwade.com.

Enjoy!

Dani

DANI WADE

RECLAIMING HIS LEGACY

ISBN-13: 978-1-335-20898-9

Reclaiming His Legacy

Copyright © 2020 by Katherine Worsham

This edition published by arrangement with Harlequin Books S.A.

For questions and comments about the quality of this book,
please contact us at CustomerService@Harlequin.com.

Harlequin Enterprises ULC
22 Adelaide St. West, 40th Floor
Toronto, Ontario M5H 4E3, Canada
www.Harlequin.com

Printed in U.S.A.

Dani Wade astonished her local librarians as a teenager when she carried home ten books every week—and actually read them all. Now she writes her own characters, who clamor for attention in the midst of the chaos that is her life. Residing in the southern United States with her husband, two kids, two dogs and one grumpy cat, she stays busy until she can closet herself away with her characters once more.

Books by Dani Wade

Harlequin Desire

Milltown Millionaires

A Bride's Tangled Vows
The Blackstone Heir
The Renegade Returns
Expecting His Secret Heir

Savannah Sisters

A Family for the Billionaire
Taming the Billionaire
Son of Scandal

Louisiana Legacies

Entangled with the Heiress
Reclaiming His Legacy

Visit her Author Profile page at Harlequin.com, or daniwade.com, for more titles.

You can also find Dani Wade on Facebook, along with other Harlequin Desire authors, at Facebook.com/harlequindesireauthors!

This book is dedicated to my son, Riley.
Thank you for making me laugh,
for challenging me to be authentic,
for each and every hug.
May you ever find something in life that you love.
Go forth and conquer!

One

"What happened to the nanny, Father?"

For a moment, Blake Boudreaux thought his father wouldn't answer. Instead Armand Boudreaux adopted the inscrutable, haughty look that matched his perfectly fitted suit, manicured hair and highly polished shoes. All of which said he wasn't obligated to give excuses to anyone. Then one perfectly trimmed brow slowly lifted and he replied with dead calm, "My traitor of a wife cleaned out her bank account. A sizable amount, I might add. I had to recoup my investment somehow."

"By firing the nanny of a sick child? Are you crazy?"

"You never had a nanny and you were just fine."

Blake could say more than a few words on that subject, but this wasn't the time or place... Not that his father would care anyway. Besides, being back inside the Boudreaux plantation house was making his skin crawl already. This place left him chilled to his core, even after all these years away. "I didn't have epilepsy. This is a serious illness. Abigail needs to be supervised. Taken care of."

"That mess is all in her head. Obviously so, or her mother wouldn't have flaked off to Europe and left her behind."

Wasn't that sympathetic of him?

"So the doctors are lying?"

"They're making a mountain out of a molehill. Really, they should do what they do best. Give her a pill that will make it all go away. It doesn't need to be more involved than that, I'm sure. As long as she takes the medicine, she'll be fine. And more importantly, she will believe its fine. That's about all its good for."

Blake knew a lot of things about his father. He was cold and autocratic, and spent his life tearing holes in the people around him. Sometimes he was subtle about it…sometimes not. But this was the first time he'd known Armand to truly jeopardize someone's life. Blake truly believed this was not something to play around with.

Abigail, Blake's half sister, was seven years old and her symptoms had been severe enough for her "flaky mother" to take her to a specialist. Of course, the minute the diagnosis had been made, she'd packed her bags and headed out to less stressful pastures.

"The doctors aren't crazy. This could be dangerous," he insisted.

"It's not as bad as they make it seem. Besides, you sound like someone who honestly cares," his father pointed out with a smirk. "Considering this is the first time I've seen your face since you told me to shove my money and my parental rights seventeen years ago, I guess I should take you seriously."

The dig wasn't unjustified. This *was* the first time Blake had set foot in his father's house since he was eighteen years old. If he had never again walked through the doors of the infamous Boudreaux plantation house, he would never have missed it. He could have continued to live in the most luxurious settings in Europe, rather than return to this arctic tundra of a house despite the sultry heat of the Louisiana summer outside.

He would never have met his father's much younger second wife, Marisa, and his then five-year-old half sister if said wife hadn't been on a trip in Germany at the same time Blake had been involved with the princess of a small, nearby principality.

That's when he'd discovered that Marisa loved to travel to exotic places and be seen by the most important people. Abigail's care was relegated to a nanny while her mother spent her days exploring her next big adventure. She'd only taken Abigail along because Armand had refused to let her leave the child at home. Marisa matched his father in narcissism, though she lacked his vindictive streak.

Blake had never thought he would ever care about

children in any capacity that had an impact on his life. His playboy reputation was widely known and accepted by all but those women who tried—and failed—to change him. Children were something that existed and were cute…as long as they belonged to someone else.

But one charming afternoon with the little girl with soft ringlets, wide brown eyes and a keen curiosity about everything around her had this playboy hooked. Luckily, Marisa had facilitated his attempts to stay in touch with his half sister until a few months ago. Blake would have had no idea about the present situation if his half sister's former nanny hadn't called out of the blue two days ago with the distressing news. Blake had rented a private jet and gone to New Orleans immediately.

Thank goodness he had an inheritance outside of his father's reach. His mother's exclusive gift had given him the chance to live a carefree life without a thought to money…or his father's opinion. The fact that he successfully supplemented that income with an avid interest in producing and distributing art was a bonus known only to him.

"I do care about Abigail," Blake finally said. Better to keep it simple than give his father any ammunition to use against him. "Someone should."

"She's weak. Life will toughen her up."

His father turned his laser-focused gaze on Blake, studying him in a way that made Blake want to squirm. He resisted the urge, of course. He was long past the point where he would allow his father to direct his actions in any way. Showing any sign of weakness would be seen as a victory by the old man, and Blake wasn't giving an inch.

"But since you're here, I might consider giving you the job."

That wasn't what Blake expected at all. "Excuse me?"

"The job of looking after her. Though you're hardly qualified for childcare, now, are you?"

At least I'm willing to try. Blake simply locked his jaw and waited. If his father was willing to about-face, there would be a price to pay. Might as well wait for the bill.

"I don't know," the older man said, fiddling with his diamond cuff links as he pretended to consider the situation. "I haven't decided if I'll let you see her at all."

A sudden tiny gasp sounded from behind a chair tucked into the far corner of the room. Unfortunately it echoed off the vaulted ceiling, and was magnified for the listeners nearby. His father's gaze swung immediately to the shadows.

"I told you to stay in your room," he yelled, his booming voice forcing Blake to suppress a wince.

A little girl slid out from behind the piece of furniture. Despite a little extra height on her, Blake would have said she was unchanged in the last two years. She had the same brown ringlet curls, though they were currently a tangled mess. The same vulnerable gaze. She hesitated before obeying, her brown eyes, flecked with green, seeming to memorize every

inch of Blake as if afraid she would never see him
again. Blake could certainly relate. His father was
just enough of a jerk to forbid him to ever see her if
he realized how much it meant to Blake.

So he hid his own emotions, gave Abigail the barest of smiles and motioned for her to go upstairs…
before she heard more from her father about what a
problem she was. Blake had grown up with a lifetime
of those abusive rants stuck in his brain. He didn't
want that for Abigail.

While her mother was here, Blake had thought
she would be protected from the harsh reality of Armand Boudreaux's judgments. Now there would be
no one in a position to protect her. The housekeeper,
Sherry, might be able to check in, but she still had a
job to do. Would that be enough?

Blake hadn't even had that much. He remembered
long, endless days when he barely saw anyone except the cook, who would fix him a plate. He'd been
healthy, but lonely. Except having his father take an
interest in him had usually meant an hour of yelling
about how horrible Blake was.

Blake couldn't allow that to happen to Abigail.
Two years ago, he never gave his terrible childhood a
second thought, but Abigail's situation was bringing
a lot of bad memories to the forefront of his brain.

Turning his gaze back to his father, he continued
as if they hadn't been interrupted. "You were saying I could help with Abigail's care?" Caution was
the name of the game here.

"Sure. You care so much about her—" Armand

narrowed his gaze on Blake, a thin smile stretching his lips. "It might be worth something for you to see her."

Oh boy. "Don't you have enough money?"

The seconds-long hesitation sent a spear of worry through Blake. Money had never been an issue for his father. Not growing up. And, Blake assumed, not now. But that hesitation made him wonder.

Then his father said, "Not money, son. *Freedom*."

A pretty significant bargaining chip for Blake. It always had been. This would not end well. "I'm not following."

His father paced back and forth across the marble floor, the click of his dress shoes echoing off the vaulted ceiling. Blake's stomach sank. This was his father's move whenever he was plotting…planning. Definitely not good.

His father paused, tapping his index finger against his bottom lip. "I think there might be a solution to this situation that will benefit us both."

Hell, no. "I know how this works. Your solutions only benefit you."

"It depends on how you look at it." His father's smile was cold. "This could definitely benefit Abigail. Isn't that what you *say* you want?"

"I never said any such thing."

"Your actions speak loud enough for you."

And he'd thought he'd shown remarkable restraint… Remaining silent would keep Blake from incriminating himself further. So he kept his trap shut and his gaze glued to the man before him. Armand fitted in so well with the sterile beauty of the Boudreaux plantation. It was his perfect backdrop.

"Yes, I believe this will definitely work. I've waited a long time for this." Armand nodded as if confirming the thought to himself. His full head of silver hair glinted in the sun from the arched window behind him. "And you're gonna give me exactly what I want."

Blake turned away, panic running through him at the thought of going back to being that eighteen-year-old boy who had no defenses against his father. But just when he thought he would stride right over to the door and disappear through it, he caught a glimpse of tangled brown hair and pink leggings at the top of the stairs.

What choice do I have?

He could report Armand for neglect, but Blake doubted that would do more than dent his father's reputation. Armand knew too many people in high places for any charges to go far. Abigail probably wouldn't even be removed from the home.

He could take her with him now, but that would probably lead to him being accused of kidnapping... and she'd end up right back home.

He needed more time, more resources...but he could not let Abigail down, even if it meant turning his own life inside out to help her. Who would have guessed this playboy would grow a conscience?

He turned back to his father. "What do you want me to do?"

With a grin that said he knew he'd gotten his way,

Armand slipped through the double doors at the far end of the room leading to his office, then returned with a file folder in his hand. Blake didn't dare look up the stairs and give away Abigail's continued presence. But he was conscious of her sitting just out of his father's line of sight.

"There is a woman here in town, Madison Landry. She has something that belongs to me. Something you will retrieve."

"Can't you get a lawyer to take care of that?"

"That route has proved…fruitless. Now it's time for a different approach."

The rare admission of failure was unheard of from his father, which piqued Blake's interest. "So you want me to convince a former…what, lover?…to return something to you?" Obviously legal channels hadn't worked, so his father didn't have a legitimate leg to stand on.

His father smirked. "Hardly." He pulled a photograph out of the file. "Have you ever heard of the Belarus diamond?"

"No." Jewels had never been a major focus for Blake.

"It's a rare, two-carat, fancy vivid blue diamond that was gifted to our family by a Russian prince before we settled in Louisiana after leaving France. When I was young and foolish, I had the diamond placed into a setting for an engagement ring. For a woman who did not deserve anything nearly so special."

Well, this was news to Blake. He studied a photograph of a brilliant blue oval-shaped jewel. "You were engaged before my mother?"

"To the daughter of a now nearly extinct family from Louisiana society, Jacqueline Landry. The engagement lasted less than a year."

"So she dumped you?"

If not, Armand would have taken steps to get back what was his before walking away.

Armand's back went ramrod straight, as if he were affronted by the assumption. His sigh indicated he had no high horse to sit on. "She made the foolish choice to leave, and took the ring with her. That diamond belongs to our family. It is mine to do with as I wish."

But not the ring? This wasn't about a piece of jewelry Armand could hand down to his children. It was about something else… Money? Pride? Surely not after all of these years.

"Then you shouldn't have given it away," Blake reasoned.

"I sent several letters through the years demanding the ring back, all of which were returned unopened."

"From my limited experience with broken engagements, that's her prerogative."

His father's snap to attention told Blake he'd touched a nerve.

"Dammit, this is not the time for your flippant sarcasm. I want that ring and I will have it." Armand smoothed down his hair and jacket in a move utterly familiar to Blake. Growing up, he'd seen it often after his father's rages. Blake steeled himself as a wave of unpleasant emotions washed over him.

"You will get it for me, Blake."

"How? You don't even know if Jacqueline's daughter still has it."

"There's never been any record of it being found or sold. Which means it's still in the family's possession somehow. You will find this woman and get it back from her. With her knowledge or without it."

"You expect me to convince her to just hand over a priceless diamond that belonged to her mother?"

"You'll find a way. I'm sure a man like you, one who has seduced and discarded numerous women through the years, will have no problem with this mission. It should be a perfect use for the very few skills you've actually cultivated in your lifetime."

Blake had to admit, that stung a little. Even if it came from his father, who wouldn't have a nice thing to say about him if he'd used his wealth to become a big-shot CEO, either. Of course, the other skills Blake had developed he kept well disguised behind the facade of his carefree lifestyle. "Those women knew the score going in."

"This one won't. And I forbid you to enlighten her." He narrowed his gaze on his son. "Until afterward, of course. If you want to tell her you stole from her to save your sister, that's your business."

Armand handed over a file with all the confidence of a man who would get his way. "Read it. Let me know."

"I can't do this." *Could he?*

"And there's one more condition," his father went on, as if Blake hadn't spoken. "Access to Abigail will be limited by me until the job is done. But afterward, you can have her all to yourself. I'll sign the paperwork to wash my hands of her, and you can give her the upbringing you claim she needs."

Bile rose in the back of Blake's throat. He wasn't sure what he'd expected when he'd walked back through the Boudreaux plantation's doors, but no part of this conversation had gone according to plan. What business did a man who'd spent his life deliberately avoiding any type of responsibility have raising a young girl with epilepsy?

As if he could read Blake's thoughts, his father smirked. "Are you sure a playboy like you is up to the challenge?"

"Sleepy?"

Madison Landry started awake, embarrassed at being caught sleeping by her boss at Maison de Jardin. "I'm so sorry," she stammered out, "I'm just not sleeping well right now."

"It's not a problem for me," Trinity Hyatt said with one of her trademark gracious smiles, "especially since you're here on your day off. Want to tell me why that is?"

Madison tried to shrug off the question with a lame excuse. "There's always plenty to do around here." And there was.

The charity, which provided a safe haven and life skills training for abused women and children, was in a constant state of managed chaos. If it wasn't laundry that needed doing, it was job applications or fund-raising or any number of things. The desk in front of her in the downstairs office was filled to overflowing with paperwork and records.

Not for anything would Madison admit she'd come over to Maison de Jardin, which shared a border with her family estate, because she needed a distraction. Not because work needed to be done.

The last thing she wanted to discuss were the sleepless nights. The memories of her father's last painful days. Dreams where she could hear him struggle to breathe with the pneumonia clouding his lungs, causing fear to tighten her own chest. Waves of gratitude over the old-fashioned doctor who would still come to the house to treat him after her father's refusal to be moved to a hospital. The stuff of her nightmares.

Though the understanding expression in Trinity's soft gaze said she probably knew already. And her boss wasn't one to shy away from the hard discussions. "Well, I hate to see you suffering from insomnia. I had the same issue after my mom died. Just couldn't turn my brain off for anything."

"That's definitely an issue," Madison agreed, fiddling with her pen as she thought back over so many sleepless nights lately. It was one of the few things Madison felt comfortable discussing. She tried distracting Trinity from any deeper issues. "Besides, it's hard to retrain yourself to sleep well after having to stay alert during the night for so long."

Only her attempt at distraction just gave her boss more fodder for discussion.

"How many years did you take care of your dad?" Trinity asked, leaning against the doorjamb.

Her gaze swept over the room with familiarity, giving Madison a momentary reprieve. After all, the office had last been Trinity's. She'd only moved up to take care of Hyatt Heights, the company started by her late husband. He and his parents had established Maison de Jardin in New Orleans when he'd been a young man. But taking over his company meant Trinity didn't have time to run the charity, too, especially after her late husband's relatives had gone to court to fight over his estate.

Madison just happened to be in the right place at the right time. She'd known Trinity since she was a teenager, coming over to the shelter to help whenever she could. Unfortunately, her dad's illness had prevented that at times. But when Trinity had to move on, she'd trusted Madison to step into the role despite her age, knowing her life experience went way beyond her years.

Trinity's perusal of her old office ended with a look straight at Madison, who squashed the urged to squirm in her seat.

Madison cleared her throat. "Ten. But the sleeping and mobility issues were only a problem for the last five or so."

"Madison," Trinity said in a voice so gentle it eased Madison's instinctive panic. "You realize that it's perfectly normal to *not* be okay. Right?"

Madison knew her answers were clipped, but the dread she'd felt for weeks was clawing at the back of her throat with each word.

Multiple sclerosis was a tough disease. One Madison didn't wish on anyone after dealing with it up close and personal. The thought of what her dad had gone through always made her sad. He'd lost his business when Madison was young, then been diagnosed with MS before losing the love of his life. But they'd had good times together, too, leaning on each other for comfort and joy.

Madison could barely respond above a whisper. "I know." With a hard mental shove, she locked all those roiling emotions away. The more she talked about them, the more power they had. It was better just to move forward. "It's really okay," she said, mentally reminding herself that her restlessness and fear and pain could be normalized. "Last night, I spent the time cleaning and reading some more of my mother's journals." After all, what else was there to do at three in the morning?

There was a gentle caution in Trinity's question. "Are you sure you're ready to clean out the house, Madison? Your father has only been gone six months."

As much as she sometimes wished it didn't, Madison was well aware that life had to go on. "The house has to go on the market soon. With only me to clean it out…" She shrugged, as if this wasn't a discussion she'd had with herself a million times over.

Shuffling the papers on the desk before her didn't distract her from the ache of knowing she would have to sell the only home she'd ever had. It was falling down around her, even after years of doing the best she could with it, but every one of her lifetime of memories involved that house somehow. Knowing she would have to part with it was only making her grief grow exponentially.

But who knew how long it would take to clean out the clutter and sort through her parents' possessions? She discovered new pockets of stuff all the time. Just a couple of months ago she'd found a collection of journals that had belonged to her mother. Reading them had brought her memory back in vivid detail. They brought her a lot of solace as she sorted through more and more stuff.

And she had no idea how she would afford to do any of the repairs the house would need, much less cosmetic work, before she put it on the market. Her job here paid her substantially better than the odd jobs she'd taken to keep her and her dad afloat after her mother's accidental death, but years of neglect had led to some significant damage in what had once been the most beautiful, stately home in New Orleans's Garden District.

Deep down, Madison just wished it was all over and done with. That the house was fixed, sold and being renovated by someone who could afford to return it to its former glory. It might hurt to rip the bandage off, but at least it would be gone.

I can only do so much...was the mantra she lived by. All of her life Madison had focused on one task at a time, because she was only one person, usually working without any help. Coming to Maison de Jardin had allowed her to be part of a team. But for much of her life, it had been her…or nobody.

"I'm so sorry, Madison."

"Don't be," she replied with a shaky smile. But at least she still remembered how to form one. "Coming to work here has been the best thing that's ever happened to me. Thank you, Trinity."

"Girl, I couldn't do it without you. Especially right now. I know the women here are in good hands. But—" She grinned. "Enough of all this emotion… I have an exciting surprise for you."

"What?" Madison welcomed the change of subject, relief easing her tense muscles.

"Your dress came in!"

For most women, the news would be exciting. For Madison, it brought on another fit of nervousness. Next week they would be attending a society fund-raising event, a first for Madison. She'd never had cause to leave her father's sickroom for such things, nor the funds. But in her new capacity as director for Maison de Jardin, it would be her job to mix and mingle with New Orleans's best and brightest. Though their legacy from Trinity's deceased husband should fund them for a long time to come, it never hurt to have support from others who could afford to help.

Thus, Madison found herself about to be presented to New Orleans high society.

A generation ago, it would have been Madison's rightful place. Her parents both came from established families that had helped found this incredible city. The last of their respective lines, the love merger should have cemented them as a power couple.

But Madison only knew this from a few stories she'd heard from her mother growing up. Her mother had been very secretive about their marriage and choice to live a more isolated life despite their prominent home in New Orleans's Garden District. Something had happened around the time of their marriage, but Madison had never been able to figure out quite what the scandal had been.

Which was why she'd been reading her mother's journals each night after finding them in one of the closed-off rooms on the upper floor of their house. Maybe there she could find some clue to how her parents had met and married. After all, stories like that might replace the sad memories she currently fought off during her sleepless nights.

Trinity took her hand and led her through the halls of Maison de Jardin to the master suite up on the second floor. It was currently empty, having been Trinity's room before she moved out when she married Michael Hyatt a mere two months ago. Michael's tragic death and Trinity's current battle over his estate left her life a little unsettled. Since Madison lived nearby for the time being, she hadn't claimed the space as hers, wanting Trinity to still feel like she had a home here if she needed it.

Laid across the pale blue bedspread was a beautiful lavender dress. Madison gasped, letting her fingers train over the soft flow of material.

"It's an unusual color for a redhead," Trinity said. "I think it's gonna be a fabulous choice."

Madison hoped so.

This was how she would be presented to society. Her stomach churned, though her nerves were a welcome distraction from her earlier grief. First impressions were a big deal. While her family name had been well known in NOLA in the past, history had slowly erased it from the current consciousness. The South still prided itself on its history, and the history of its families, but money stood for a lot more. It was the way of the world. Madison knew that and knew she couldn't change it. With her father's illness, her family had drained its coffers until all they had was social security and what little she could eke out from various odd jobs. Her father's health meant she couldn't go to work full-time.

She had to remember, this was her job now. Making a good impression would allow her to be helpful to the charity—now and in the future. But that didn't ease her nerves.

Should she back out now? Give in to the fear and tell Trinity she would need someone who could better handle this part of the job?

"Let's try it on!" Trinity exclaimed, her excitement puncturing Madison's growing fears.

When she stepped back into the bedroom suite after changing, Madison didn't recognize herself in the mirror. The bodice was fitted, with only one strap made out of fabric flowers that went over her left shoulder. Multiple layers of chiffon allowed the skirt to swing around her legs to right above her knees.

"A killer set of strappy heels and you're all set."

Madison chuckled. "Let's just hope I don't break a leg in them."

"You'll be fine. It just takes practice."

Madison brushed her hands down over the gown, learning the shape with her shaking fingers. She didn't even look like herself. It was hard to take it all in.

"We can do your hair like this," Trinity said as she lifted Madison's mass of thick auburn tresses to the top of her head. "With some drop earrings and curls."

"I feel kind of like Cinderella," Madison said with an unsteady laugh.

"Well, maybe you will meet a Prince Charming at the ball. It's really just a good ol' New Orleans party, but you know good and well there will be dancing. Won't that be fun?"

The very concept was foreign to a practical girl like Madison, but the transformation hinted at in the mirror egged her on. After all, she'd never been someone who backed away from what needed to be done. Ever. "I could use a little fun."

Trinity gave her an exaggerated wide-eyed look in the mirror.

"Okay," Madison conceded, "I need quite a bit of fun."

"As long as it's safe."

And requires nothing that makes me think too hard. In fact, a Prince Charming might be a little too complicated for her right now. Her life had always been and continued to be full of responsibilities and organization and obligations… She needed some space from all of that.

Madison smiled at herself in the mirror.

And who knew? Maybe she could find a *Prince for Now* to have some fun with. A girl could dream, right?

Two

What the hell was he doing here?

Blake should have been perfectly at home at the party being held at the home of one of Louisiana's most famous power couples. It was the type of event where people with money gathered to discuss local gossip and politics, and generally impress others with their money and intelligence…or lack thereof. Blake frequented many such parties all across Europe. The only change was the language and food. The people were mostly the same.

While he usually anticipated getting lucky at such parties, he'd never gone to one for the express purpose of initiating a one-night stand.

Yes, casual sex was a part of his lifestyle, but the women he spent time with were always on the same page. He made sure of that up front. The fact that the only plan he could come up with—in terms of feasibility and expediency—was to get into the Landry home by way of a one-night stand brought on a completely foreign feeling of shame.

But for Abigail, he'd do what he had to.

Hell, even reporting Armand for neglect wasn't an option. His father had more than one city official in his pocket. Besides, could he risk the possibility that Abigail might be forced into foster care before he could get everything worked out? At least at home there was a sympathetic housekeeper to keep an eye on her. Sherry couldn't be with her all the time, but she was always nearby and looking out for Abigail. At least, that's what Blake had gathered from their phone conversations. Given the odds of her ending up some place worse than his father's house, Blake knew his best bet was to get the diamond as soon as absolutely possible.

So, as uncomfortable as the idea made him, his only choice seemed to be seducing Madison Landry to fulfill his father's demands…unless he wanted to resort to breaking and entering.

It hadn't taken him long to spot the woman he sought in the crowd, though she appeared much younger than he'd anticipated.

Even in the photographs in the file, she hadn't looked quite as old as her twenty-six years. Maybe it was her pale complexion or the dusting of freckles across her nose that she hadn't bothered to hide for tonight's occasion. But somehow he'd expected the hard life that had been briefly chronicled in the file to show on her face.

She'd also spent most of her time here barely speaking and rarely venturing from the table she was standing near. He'd been anticipating someone eager to display herself on the marriage market, rather than the quiet woman he saw before him. After all, she was young, single and had too hard of a life to be a party girl. She wasn't dancing, though she moved slightly to the music as if it intrigued her. There was no steady round of interested men introducing themselves. Certainly no flirting.

She appeared to be a species he had no experience with.

He had enough confidence to approach her while she was still surrounded by her friends. But now it looked like he wouldn't have to. She'd just returned from the restroom to her table alone, looking longingly out on the dance floor. A young woman who needed to have some fun...and Blake was the perfect partner in crime.

Glancing down at the napkin in his hand, he grinned. Now he had an interesting opening to approach her.

Blake crossed over to the table and paused beside Madison's chair. She glanced up, then did the double take he was used to. Her eyes widened as she got a good look at him, though she quickly tried to mask her reaction. He'd never been uncomfortable knowing he'd dressed to impress—but for some reason he was tonight; it made him feel like a used car salesman.

"Hello," he said simply.

"Hi there." Her smile wasn't quite firm at the edges.

Then she glanced around as if he surely must be looking for someone else. But he wasn't. Blake knew exactly who he was meeting tonight.

Slowly he slid the napkin in front of her on the table and gave her a moment to get a good look. Her brows went up, then she leaned in for a closer look. Step One accomplished.

He'd made a sketch of her on the white scrap. Her face was in profile, and dead accurate, though the drawing lacked the vibrant color of her auburn hair and the multihued strings of lights decorating the large room.

He pitched his voice slightly louder to be heard over the music. "A woman this beautiful shouldn't be sitting on the sidelines."

The muscles in her throat worked as if she had to swallow a couple of times before she answered. "Is that a remark about my physical appearance or your artistic prowess?"

"Both?" he answered, surprised at her response. Most women would have gushed over the gift or been flattered by his remarks. He'd never been questioned over a drawing before.

Despite that, she rubbed her finger over the edges of the sketch. Finally she looked up with a small smile that seemed genuine. "How long did it take you to draw this?"

He shrugged. "About five minutes."

"At least you aren't too invested as a stalker," she said, raising a single brow as if in challenge.

Blake was shocked enough to laugh. Definitely not what he'd expected. Neither was her voice. On the deep side, slightly husky, it evoked images of mystery and sex. The opposite of her young, bright presence.

She ducked her face down for a moment, before glancing up at him through thick lashes. "I probably wasn't supposed to say that out loud."

"Definitely not." But she could keep talking all she wanted.

"I knew I'd never fit in here."

On their surface, the words could be taken as if she were teasing, just making polite conversation, but the way she worried her bottom lip with the edge of her teeth told him otherwise. "First time?" he asked.

She nodded, causing the colored lights to reflect off the glorious red of her hair. Blake had the sudden urge to see it down around her shoulders, rather than pulled back from the heart shape of her face. His lips suddenly felt dry. "Me, too," he murmured.

To his surprise, she leaned a little closer. "So you're not from around here?"

"Yes—" Suddenly the music cut out, making Blake's voice sound loud. "Yes, I am from here, but it's been a while. Care to be new together?"

Again her teeth pressed against the fullness of

her lower lip, causing blood to rush into the curve as she released it. "My friends will be back soon."

Blake ignored the subtle rejection. "Good, then they can watch me *not* stalk you on the dance floor."

Suddenly the music started up again, this time with an exuberant trumpet player in the lead.

He moved in closer to make himself heard. Leaning toward her ear, he asked, "Would you like to dance?"

Her breath caught, trapped inside her throat as she swallowed once more. Then her body gave a quick shiver, though it was far from cold in the room. Blake should be grateful for her reaction, this confirmation that she wasn't immune to him, but instead he felt a strange mixture of grim determination and melting heat low in his belly. Did she feel the same attraction as he found trickling through his unprepared consciousness?

Madison's gaze swung longingly toward the dance floor. Until now, the lively sound of jazz tunes had filled the air all night but she hadn't once approached the dance floor.

"Well, I don't think so."

To his shock, she pulled back a couple of inches. "What's the matter? Part of coming to a dance party is to dance."

"I think people come to parties for a lot of different reasons," she said, glancing down as she ran her finger over the edge of the drawing once more. "To socialize, to drink, to eat, to be seen…" She paused, and he swore he saw a flush creep over her cheeks, even in the dim light.

A woman who still blushed? Blake couldn't remember the last time he'd dealt with one of those. Before he could confirm it, she glanced the other way. Maybe to look for her friends? Maybe to hide the evidence?

He wasn't sure, but part of him, the part that had been watching her tonight, wanted to know for sure. In fact, the more he watched, the more he wanted to know. And that interest made him even more uncomfortable with what he was doing here tonight.

"I'm Blake Boudreaux, by the way," he said.

To his relief, no recognition showed in her expression.

"I'm Madison." She seemed to relax a little before she asked, "Did you move away for work?"

Oh, she was gonna make him earn that dance, wasn't she? "More like life management."

"Seriously?"

"Yes. Leaving allowed me to have a life." He softened his unexpected answer with as charming a grin as he could muster.

Madison cocked her head to the side, awakening an urge to kiss her delicate chin. He straightened just a little. "I'm just visiting long enough to handle a family issue."

She nodded, the move containing an odd wisdom considering her youth. "Those aren't easy."

"Never, but they are the reason we drink and have fun."

The laugh that came from her surprised him. No giggles for this girl. Instead she gave a full-bodied laugh that made tingles run down his spine. She didn't try to hide her enjoyment of his little joke or keep her response polite.

"So how about that dance?"

Suddenly a strange look came across her face—a combination of surprise and panic and almost fear. This time her retreat was obvious. Blake sat stunned as she mumbled, "I… I don't think that's a good idea. I mean…" She waved her hand in front of her as if to erase her response but inadvertently bumped her drink and knocked it over.

"Oh, my. I'm so sorry."

"It's okay." Blake wasn't sure why, but he reached out to grasp her hands in his. "It's okay, Madison."

She started to smile, but then her face contorted and she jerked her hands away. "Good night," she said, then turned on her heel and ran into the crowd.

Blake stared for a moment in confusion. They'd seemed to be having a good time. She wasn't as comfortable with men coming up to her as he'd expected, but she hadn't shown any signs of hating him during the conversation. What had gone wrong? This was not at all how he'd expected tonight to turn out. But then again, not much about Madison had turned out how he'd expected.

Honestly, this hadn't happened since he'd passed his eighteenth birthday, and he had no idea how to handle it. Something had spooked her. Should he leave it for tonight and try to find another way in?

Thoughts of Abigail and what might happen to her in the amount of time it might take him to find another opening into Madison's life had his heart pounding hard in his chest. He clenched his fists. He would not let her down.

Reaching out, he righted the now-empty wine glass. The small amount of liquid that had been inside had already been absorbed by the tablecloth. Next to the stain lay the napkin with Madison's sketch on it and a small lavender bag.

A bag? As the realization hit that it must be Madison's, so did a renewed sense of purpose. A one-night stand might not be an option, but at least he could arrange a date? It would afford him a chance to impress her and possibly find another way into her house to do some digging.

Plunging into the crowd, Blake didn't give himself time to think or plan. Halfway across the room he saw Madison and her friends near the door, speaking to the hosts as if they were about to leave. Adrenaline quickened his step as he realized his window of opportunity was closing.

The opportunity to find the diamond and save his sister. To understand more about the unusual woman with her emerald green eyes. To explore the strange feelings she called up inside of him.

Blake called out her name when she and her friends were just steps from vanishing through the door into the warm Southern night.

"Madison."

She glanced over her shoulder, her eyes widening

as she saw him. She turned back to her friends, but Blake wasn't going to let that stop him. He stepped into the circle without an invitation.

"Madison, I believe this is yours." He held out the lavender bag.

"Oh, yes." She frowned as she looked at the offering. "Yes, I'm so sorry—"

"I thought you might need it," he said, cutting off her words, which seemed to just compound her awkwardness.

"Thank you so much."

He glanced at the couple standing with them, but the woman simply gave a composed smile. "We'll meet you at the car, Madison," she said and they turned to leave.

Madison took the bag from his outstretched hand, then fiddled with the strap for a moment. "I really do appreciate this," she murmured.

Luckily, they were far enough away from the dance floor that he could hear her. "Look, Madison. I think maybe I came on too strong back there."

"No. No, it wasn't you. It's me. I'm just not used to—" She waved her hand around them, "Please don't think you did anything wrong."

He could almost feel her need to leave as the feeling came over her. Something about her body language told him she was ready to run. He couldn't let that happen.

"Tell you what, how about you make it up to me?"

Her gaze flicked up to his, and he gave her a teasing smile. "Or rather, how can I get a second chance…an opportunity to get to know you when I don't have to yell to be heard?"

Her muscles relaxed and she smiled, just a little. Why did that smile feel like a big victory?

So let's try this again… "Where can I pick you up?"

"Why in the world did I agree to this?"

Madison looked around at the array of clothes that she'd brought over to try on for Trinity. Never in her life had she done this. She'd never been the girl to worry over what she wore or what her makeup looked like or how other people perceived her outward physical appearance. Because her life didn't have anything to do with that.

It was about helping others and doing what needed to be done for her daddy. Not clothes and shoes. Her daddy had never cared about any of those things. And neither had Trinity. It was easier to do their job in jeans or yoga pants.

Even her mother's journals provided no blueprint for how to date. Madison had found them oddly lacking in information from before her marriage. There were a few comments about a happy childhood but nothing about dating or her engagement.

Right now, it was easier to focus on clothes than to wonder whether she could sit across from a man as suave and charismatic as Blake Boudreaux and be comfortable and happy and…have fun?

The women at Maison de Jardin were grateful for

a helping hand and a friend. That was what made Madison feel fulfilled.

Wasn't it? She had to admit to an unfamiliar restlessness since her daddy had died six months ago. It wasn't that she didn't enjoy helping people. But there was an aching need for something a little *more*. Something only hinted at on the nights she sang at a local nightclub—a hobby that she could indulge now that her father was gone. The pure enjoyment of losing herself in things that didn't require her to meet someone else's needs. That didn't require her to work, to figure out how to fix things. She'd been doing that stuff all her life.

Maybe it was the extra space in her life now that her last living relative was gone. Maybe it was her age, and the realization that most young women were starting to settle down or already had by now. Maybe it was just a quirk of her overactive imagination. But for once, she simply needed enjoyment without any responsibility attached.

Would she find that with Blake? Everything about that man made her nervous and excited and tingly in ways she'd never felt before. He made her feel emotions that weren't exactly comfortable enough to be called fun. He made her feel *too much*. Especially when he moved in close, smelling spicy and exuding heat.

Just thinking about it made her heart thud hard against her ribs.

She hadn't imagined two people could have that much chemistry outside of a bedroom. He made her think of magic and sin and heat all mixed together in the air. Incredible.

Which only made her more awkward, more anxious than she'd ever felt. Her life was built on a definition of success that had become uniquely hers through the years. Not money or fancy cars or expensive clothes, but days and hours and moments of achievement through sheer determination, hard work and action. Not this uncertainty that made her feel paralyzed.

"What am I doing, Trinity?" she asked, unable to resist nibbling at the inside of her lower lip. "Why did I say yes to this?"

But she knew why. It had been a combination of that tingly excitement and the fact that he'd tracked her down and given her purse back. She'd hastily surrendered her phone number, then rushed out the door with burning cheeks and butterflies in her stomach.

"Everything will be fine," her friend assured her. "Did he tell you what y'all were gonna do?"

"No," Madison huffed. "He said he wanted it to be a surprise. All I have is an address and that's about it."

"Which I know is driving you crazy. You're nothing if not prepared."

Trinity knew her too well. "The mystery should be perfect. It should help me step out of my comfort zone. Instead—" Madison pressed her fist against her stomach.

"I know, love." Trinity gave her a quick hug. "What's the address?"

Madison picked up her phone to review Blake's texts. "Looks like it's somewhere down near the river."

"Well, meeting him there is a smart move." Trinity's lips twisted in a small grimace, confirming Madison's belief that she needed to keep her own vehicle nearby. Better to take precautions and be safe than sorry later. "I guess working in this place makes me extra cautious."

Me, too. Madison had tried to be a modern woman—also something she didn't have a lot of experience in—assuring Blake she could get herself where they were going. After all, what did she really know about him besides chemistry? Except now the lack of information made her feel even more ill-prepared for the night ahead.

The array of clothes before her included a relatively small number of articles from her own closet and a few she'd just spent a meager part of her salary on at an upscale secondhand store. "So we'll be near the river, right?" she asked herself more than Trinity. With an impatient sigh, she grabbed a new pair of jean shorts and a casual blouse and forced herself to dress without thinking any more about how she looked.

Trinity offered an understanding smile. "If you need anything, keep your cell phone on you. I'll come get you if you call. No matter what time."

"I will," Madison said as she tried to breathe through her nerves.

"Text me anyway when you get there so I know everything is okay."

This time Madison smiled. "Yes, Mama."

But she was very grateful for Trinity's offer when she arrived at the address and found herself near a marina. She walked along the worn planks of the dock until she found Blake waiting for her halfway down. Next to him in the slip was a very smooth, very elegant boat.

Embarrassed heat washed over her immediately. Only sheer determination kept her feet walking toward him. He was dressed in a designer polo and dress pants, standing next to the nicest boat she'd ever seen—even on television. She tugged down on the hem of her shirt, wishing she'd opted for a summer dress at the very least.

What the heck was she doing here? she asked herself for the bazillionth time that evening.

Blake didn't seem to notice. "Good evening," he said smoothly.

Madison drew her gaze away from the craft, realizing her mouth had dropped open…just a little. But all that gleaming chrome sure was pretty…and way above her pay grade.

"I'm glad to see you made it," Blake said, as if he hadn't noticed her gawking.

Madison could barely meet his eyes. This wasn't a situation she knew how to handle or fix or arrange. What should she say? *Nice boat?* Was it even called that? Or was it a small yacht? *Ugh.* "I'll admit, I almost backed out." *Dang it.* Why did she say that?

But Blake chuckled. "I guess I understand. After all, I'm practically a stranger. Though why you wouldn't want to spend the evening with someone as heroic as me…"

"Heroic?"

With a sheepish grin, he offered a hand to steady her as she stepped onto the craft. "I did return a missing purse."

"That hardly qualifies," she scoffed.

"A guy can hope, right?"

She raised a brow at his begging puppy dog expression, then forced herself to glance around the boat. "The question is, can you pilot this thing without breaking it?"

"You'd be surprised how smooth she is in the water. A captain's dream."

Something about the way he said the words sent a tingle along her spine. The good kind…not the afraid-he's-a-serial-killer kind. To distract herself, she hurriedly took a picture of the boat's name on the prow and texted it to Trinity, much to his bemusement. Even though Blake didn't give her any creepy vibes, she wasn't taking any chances…and he needed to know that.

"A girl can't be too careful," she said with a shrug. "After all, if you are secretly a serial killer and I disappear tonight, at least my friends will know where to start looking."

His shocked expression made her laugh. Normally, Madison never censored herself when it came to laughter. There'd been too many sad times in her life for her not to cherish every happy moment. But here, on this beautiful boat with a beautiful man, her full-bodied laugh suddenly seemed loud, obnoxious. She quickly smothered it.

"That's actually pretty smart."

To her surprise, he didn't seem offended that she might think he was dangerous. She hoped that proved he could handle the quirks that made Madison who she was. Not that she should care. She should have the attitude that if he didn't like her, she could easily walk away.

This was about fun. Not relationships or happily-ever-afters.

So why did her hand in his feel much more important than that?

Blake had clearly spared no expense when it came to tonight. The boat itself was brand-new, with a lot of bells and whistles from what she could tell. It had a large deck, covered access below and several leather-upholstered chairs in the upstairs driving area. It was the on-water equivalent of a luxury car.

Blake cast off, then joined her in the chairs up front. Now it was just the two of them. Maybe she should be happy that there wasn't a captain to navigate and watch their every move all night. She wasn't actually sure if that would have made her happy or not.

Only twenty minutes into this date and settling down seemed impossible. Blake guided the boat smoothly out of the slip and down the channel to where the shore spread out before them. The boat practically glided on the glassy surface.

At this time of year, the breeze at night was cool and comforting, a relief from the midday heat. A recent rain had lowered the humidity, though Madison knew from experience that in a couple weeks it would be uncomfortable no matter what time of day without a breeze and a cold drink.

That was life in the South.

Blake picked up speed as they gained open water, which was when the first bit of uneasiness hit Madison's stomach. Her focus turned inward as she tried to figure out the source. Maybe her nerves? After all, she had experienced plenty of anxiety over the past few days. No, this was something else. Something she couldn't quite put her finger on.

The queasiness rose with each passing minute, forcing Madison to swallow once or twice. She tried to concentrate on the feel of the wind on her skin, praying that the feeling would pass. Of all the things she'd anticipated tonight, feeling sick was not one.

Blake slowed, then stopped the boat out in the middle of the glassy gray water. The wake rocked the boat, sparking a quick surge of nausea. Madison breathed in deeply, then let it out slowly. Maybe she'd be better now that the boat had stopped.

Blake smiled over at her. "Good?"

She nodded with what was hopefully a steady smile. The last thing she wanted was a double helping of embarrassment tonight.

"I'll set up dinner then."

Madison didn't move as Blake made his way to the back. At the press of a button, a portion of the deck floor retracted and a table rose out of the depths. *Well.* She guessed they wouldn't be eating off paper plates from their laps, would they?

She didn't have a lot of experience eating outdoors with formal silverware. More like fast-food wrappers and brown paper napkins.

Madison turned back toward the front of the boat, pretending to be absorbed in the view of the water. But her stomach continued to churn. What should she do?

Ask to go back? The thought of that trip had bile backing up into her throat. She definitely couldn't eat right now. So she simply breathed and prayed whatever this was would go away.

To her relief, the unease in her stomach subsided. She gave herself another minute, then two, but the ticking clock in her head told her he would start to wonder what was going on if she kept delaying. Finally Madison stood to make her way to the back of the boat. The world seemed to tilt as she walked, even though she could swear the boat wasn't rocking. What was wrong with her?

"I'm about ready," Blake said as she approached. Then he looked up from his task. "Are you okay?"

She tried to smile. She really did. Then she glanced down at the table and saw an open container of what appeared to be chicken or crab salad. Two seconds later, she was hanging over the edge of the boat to empty her stomach.

Three

"Are you okay now?" Blake asked.

The ultra-pale cast to Madison's skin worried him. Her freckles stood out even in the dim light from the dock. They'd made it back but the last thirty minutes had been a strain, as he knew the very thing he was doing to quickly get them to land was the thing that was making her sick. It had never occurred to him that she would suffer motion sickness.

He was used to drama like crying, yelling and feigned illness. One look at Madison, with her trembling and careful movements, convinced him this was real. His chest went heavy, filling with an unfamiliar mixture of responsibility and regret.

"No," Madison croaked, her hands tightening around the edge of the dock where she now sat. She swallowed hard enough for him to see. "Actually, I'm good. Just let me not move for a while."

"I'm sorry." Her sheer desperate need to stay still made his own stomach twist. Having ridden everything from a camel to a fighter jet in the name of adventure, Blake could only relate through sympathy. "Why didn't you warn me that you suffered from motion sickness?"

She cracked one eyelid open to peek at him. Even her brilliant green eyes seemed a paler color. "I didn't know. I've never been on a boat before."

That explained that. For the second time since meeting her, Blake found himself in the minor role of rescuer. Without an instructor in sight… "I'm gonna lock everything down. Will you be okay for a few minutes?"

She nodded but didn't speak. Blake left her to get her bearings on the dock while he secured the yacht and packed up their uneaten dinner.

He wasn't sure whether to laugh or rage at his current situation. His only thought when he'd chosen this adventure had been to impress her. He knew she didn't have a lot of money and probably had never seen a vehicle like this one. Add in the reflection of a full moon on the water at night. Instant romance! That was as far as he'd gotten.

He'd been searching for the quick and easy route to accomplish his goal of getting into the house. And maybe the current situation afforded him the perfect opportunity. He could kill two birds with one stone. By taking her home and watching over her, he could make sure she didn't suffer any ill effects from the motion sickness and get some time to search the house. The longer he spent with Madison, the more sleeping with her to accomplish his plan seemed wrong. Madison wasn't a casual girl and he simply couldn't treat her that way.

His frustration sparked as he thought back over the last few days and his father's refusal to let him see Abigail. He'd been worried about how she was, and anxious to do something the old man would see as "progress" so that maybe he could check on her. But looking over at Madison on the steady wooden planks, sunk in on herself to ease the pain in her stomach, made him feel guilty for that, as well.

Blake finished securing the boat, then stepped up onto the dock. "Here," he said, offering both his hands to help her up, "let's get you home."

"Oh, right." Madison pushed her hair back behind one ear. Was her grimace one of discomfort or embarrassment? "You don't have to do that. If you'll just call me a car…"

Blake scoffed. He may be a lot of things, but he wasn't the type of man to send a sick woman home all by herself. Besides, he still had a job to do. "Absolutely not. I'll take you home. Then we'll both know you're safe." He thought back to her insistence that she meet him here. "I promise I'll take you straight to your house."

With great reluctance, Madison put her hands in his and let him lift her to her feet. He waited a moment to make sure she was steady before letting go.

He held her hands just long enough to feel the tremble in them. Was she nervous? Was it him? Or something else?

Part of him was intrigued at the myriad emotions she'd shown tonight. Most women just put the best face on things, presenting him with a facade. But not this one—she was very real.

And overly quiet as they started the drive back to New Orleans proper. Blake had to admit he found himself at a loss.

Which reminded him of exactly where he was and what he was doing. He glanced over at the woman in the seat next to him, who had her gaze trained solidly out the window. She probably was embarrassed by all of this, whereas he was completely focused on his own emotions and complications.

So he softened his voice when he said, "What's the address, Madison?"

He knew exactly where she lived. But taking her straight there would give away too much. Instead, he'd play this out like he knew nothing about her other than what she'd told him. Then he'd go to work on plan B.

"Just take me to Maison de Jardin."

The husky quality of her voice only heightened the panic racing in his veins. Nope, that wasn't a good idea.

"Are you sure? Wouldn't you be more comfortable in your own bed?"

She immediately shook her head. "No," she snapped. Surprise had him gripping the steering wheel a little tighter. So she was more spirited than he'd thought at first. As he remained silent, she squirmed just a bit, causing her seat to squeak in the quiet. He glanced over at her, but she continued to face the window.

After letting the silence stretch out for a while, he took a deep breath and said, "Look, I just don't want you to be alone and sick." And that was true, despite his currently conflicted emotions and motives. "This is my fault. Let me drive you to your house. I'll stay with you until you feel better...rest will help."

Please let this work.

The barest sounds of a sniffle caused more panic to shoot through him. But another quick glance at her showed no evidence of tears. He'd dealt with a lot of insincere waterworks through the years, but something about the rawness of Madison's demeanor right now took it to a whole other level he wasn't sure how to handle.

"Just take me to Maison de Jardin. My friend Trinity is there this evening. She'll watch over me."

He felt a wave of disappointment. He actually wanted to be there with Madison. To make this better—though he had no clue how to do that. But he wanted to be there in a way that had nothing to do with his mission. At all.

Remember Abigail... Remember why you're here...

Right.

What could he do to salvage this? He glanced over at Madison, who was in almost total darkness.

True sickness wasn't something he had any experience with. What should he do?

He stewed for a bit, tapping his finger against the steering wheel. By her deep and even breathing, he guessed she'd fallen asleep. Probably the best thing for her.

As soon as the lights of New Orleans appeared in front of them, Blake came up with plan B. Madison slept as he found the local coffee shop he wanted, and locked her inside the car. After a few minutes, he was back. Madison stirred when the internal lights flicked on.

"Where are we?" she asked.

"Not far from the house," he assured her. "I stopped to get you something for your stomach. It probably shouldn't be empty."

She glanced at the cup and frowned. "I don't think coffee is a good idea."

"It's not coffee. It's ginger lemon tea. Supposed to help settle an upset stomach."

Slowly she reached out for the cup, as if scared to believe him. "Thank you. I wouldn't have thought of that."

"Don't be impressed," he said, brushing it off. "You have just witnessed the extent of my knowledge of medicine."

She chuckled, ending with a sigh. Maybe he'd salvaged something of tonight.

A few minutes later, he pulled the car into the circular drive of Maison de Jardin, which he knew bordered her own family land. The house was lit up, assuring Blake that someone was inside.

He unbuckled his seat belt. "Let me just—"

Before he could finish, she had unstrapped herself and was out the door. "No need. Thanks, Blake."

Then the door slammed and she made a quick but unsteady trip to the front door. Blake remained frozen as she unlocked it and slipped inside. Before she did, he caught how the lights along the sidewalk glinted off the wet trails on her cheeks. So much for plan B. He thought about her having someone to look after her, then thought about Abigail, wondering if she was okay tonight.

Would he even be allowed a plan C?

"Oh, Lord. We are in trouble now."

Madison looked over her shoulder to see Trinity and one of the tenants, Tamika, come into the kitchen at Maison de Jardin. She wanted to grin at Trinity's facetious comment but instead turned back to the stand mixer on the granite counter to hide her embarrassment. She was nothing if not predictable. Another strike against her.

"Don't judge," Madison said as she continued adding flour to the mixture. "Besides, everyone benefits."

"Tell that to my waistline," Tamika complained.

"It's totally worth it," Trinity said.

Her boss at the charity completely understood where Madison was coming from. After several years of working together, she could usually recognize when Madison needed some downtime. And showing up here last night after her disaster of a date certainly qualified.

Trinity had been helping out the night before with some budgeting work, which thankfully meant Madison hadn't had to take Blake up on his offer. But she suspected that Trinity hadn't wanted to be at her deceased husband's mansion across town, hounded by memories of her best friend and the business consultant hired to make her an acceptable heir to Michael Hyatt's business empire.

One of Madison's indulgences was to bake in the kitchen at the grand house. She could bake at home, but there were a lot of sad memories associated with her house, her kitchen. It had always been depressing to make micro versions of her father's favorite sweets, because there were only two of them to cook for, and there was barely anything in the cabinets.

Here in Maison's kitchen with its original brick walls, she could focus on the peacefulness of cooking for people who appreciated it. All the amenities didn't hurt, either.

Trinity peeked over Madison's shoulder at the batch already cooling on the counter. "Chocolate chip! My favorite!"

"I'm glad I could help," Madison mumbled.

Tamika said, "I should've known you'd be here baking after your experience yesterday. I guess residual nausea kept you from starting sooner."

Madison whirled around, slapping her hands on her hips. Flour dust floated into the air. "Who told you about that?"

Tamika's eyes went wide. "I guess a little birdie told me," she said before glancing over at Trinity.

Great! The humiliation of her failed date would be all over the building by noon, less than twenty-four hours since the debacle. Word spread fast. Madison gave Trinity a pointed stare.

Her friend had a chagrined look on her face. "Sorry! I was worried about you."

"*We* were worried about you," Tamika corrected. "That's why we're down here now instead of waiting until the cookies are completely done. Besides, we thought you might need somebody to talk to after those new posts."

"What posts?" Madison asked, confused.

Tamika shook her cell phone. "Your boy is the subject of today's *New Orleans Secrets and Scandals* blog."

Trinity groaned. "No, please, no more gossip!"

"Don't blame the messenger," Tamika said with a shrug.

Trinity stomped over to the fridge. "Right about now I could use a gallon of wine."

Unfortunately for her, the charity didn't allow alcohol on the premises. But Madison could fully sympathize. The anonymous owner of the *Secrets and Scandals* blog was in the process of making Trinity's life hell. The site posted all kinds of lies about Trinity's relationship with her late husband and questioned her involvement in his death. There had even been posts digging into Trinity's abusive childhood.

The popular blog had made Trinity's current sticky situation even more complicated.

Madison wished she could help her friend as she sought to learn everything she could from the business consultant the company had hired to make Trinity a better candidate to run the businesses. She knew Trinity was afraid of losing the court case Michael's relatives had initiated to take the estate from her. Trinity didn't discuss it too much, but Madison had a feeling the situation with the consultant, who was living in the Hyatt mansion, had taken a personal turn that had Trinity more than a little unsettled.

When Tamika handed over her phone, Madison couldn't stop her gaze from scanning down the post. Its headline blared, Playboy Home for Good? Various salacious tidbits jumped out at her from there: *Last seen romancing a Greek princess... Making a splash in Rio de Janeiro...* Photographs of him looking like a Scandinavian prince with a blonde model in a bikini...

Feeling a little sick, Madison handed the phone back. That last picture especially left her feeling like a complete washout as a woman. Blake had spent his life surrounded by gorgeous women who were obviously more on her level...and could actually ride in a yacht without losing their lunch. Heck, they probably owned yachts themselves.

What in the world had he been doing with a down-on-her-luck charity director from New Orleans?

"This guy really lived it up in Europe," Tamika crowed. "He's been spotted skiing in the Alps with beautiful women, on all the best beaches, at all the fancy parties. And he doesn't seem to have a day job, so he's got to be loaded."

"Hey, he sounds like a perfect guy to just have fun with," Trinity mumbled around a bite of cookie.

Madison glared at Trinity for a second, who simply shrugged. Bitterness built up in her throat, roughening her voice as she said, "I have no idea what he was looking for on a date with someone like me, but I'm pretty sure it wasn't me hanging over the side of his boat vomiting. I seriously doubt I'll ever hear from Blake Boudreaux again."

Madison stared morosely down into the second batch of chocolate chip cookie dough, hating that she cared so much about this…hating that she couldn't shake it off…hating that she didn't seem to be the type of woman who could just have fun and not care when things went wrong.

Then she heard a slight giggle from her left, then from her right. She glanced up to find her friends desperately struggling to hold in the laughter. "I'm sorry," Trinity said. "But the visual your words call to mind is just…"

Tamika couldn't hold back any longer and burst out in laughter. Madison realized what she'd said and started to smile…then giggle…then laugh. The image of her hanging over the railing, backside in the air, while a sexy, incredibly rich man watched her ralph over the side of his yacht… If she didn't laugh, she was gonna cry.

Eventually they were all indulging in full-on belly

laughs. A sense of gratitude for these good friends who understood her and weren't afraid of a quirky sense of humor warmed her up. All too soon, they were down to a few chuckles and wiping the tears from their faces as they indulged in another spoonful of dough.

"Thanks, guys," Madison said as she tried to catch her breath. "I needed that."

But as she slowly chewed a few chocolate chips, savoring the burst of flavor against her tongue, she sobered. What had a man like that been doing with her? He was obviously sophisticated, and according to the post, he'd been with plenty of women. Model types. Nothing like Madison's red hair and freckles.

Why had he picked the least likely woman at the party to ask on a date?

"Sometimes I wonder if I was being punked the night we met." And yesterday. Except she wasn't anyone anymore. No one would care enough to read about *her*.

Trinity scoffed. "Of course not! You're a bright, attractive woman…"

"With a tendency to fatten up everyone around you," Tamika said with a saucy grin.

"We won't mention that," Madison mumbled.

Trinity raised her voice. "Who bakes the best chocolate chip cookies around…"

Not to be outdone, Tamika added, "Along with chocolate chip Bundt cakes, macaroons, apple fritters…"

"So I like to feed people. So what?"

The teasing felt good, though. Madison had gone a long time feeling alone and unappreciated. Not that her daddy hadn't loved her, but she'd been taking care of him so long that it had become more habit than anything for him to say thank-you. She knew how precious it was to have people in her life who loved her, and she made sure she let them know. Even if it was just by delivering a plate of brownies.

Here, in this kitchen, was the place she'd felt most welcome in her lifetime. That was the most important thing. Not some guy she'd just met and embarrassed herself in front of.

Her phone lit up just then, causing her to glance over at it. Blake's name flashed on the screen. "I thought for sure I'd deleted that number..." she mumbled, remembering her middle-of-the-night intention.

That was wishful thinking. After all, it wasn't like she had that many numbers in her phone. She stared at it, trying to decide what to do.

Tamika leaned over the counter for a look. "Girl, he is interested! You'd better answer that."

With the girls goading her on, Madison reached out and connected the call. The phone was chilly against her ear as she gathered the courage to speak. "Hello," she croaked.

"Hi, Madison."

Wow. How could just hearing that deep voice make her chest ache for what could have been? If only she were a different type of person. The kind who went with the flow instead of diving deep into the tide.

"Uh, hi."

"How are you feeling?"

"Fine." Could she be any more lame? "I mean, everything's good. Just some motion sickness." That she hoped never to experience again. "Boats are definitely not for me," she said, trying to laugh it off.

A glance over at Trinity and Tamika made her cringe. They weren't even pretending to not eavesdrop. Instead they both nibbled on warm cookies, watching while she agonized over what to say.

"I don't blame you," Blake said, then paused. After a long minute of silence, he went on. "Listen, I wondered if you wanted to go out again tomorrow night. Something completely on land this time."

Madison worried the inside of her bottom lip, trying to decide what to do. Even though they couldn't hear him, Trinity had a slightly skeptical look on her face. Tamika, on the other hand, was giving her the thumbs-up. For someone who came to Maison de Jardin after being in an abusive relationship, Tamika had managed to maintain her belief that a happily-ever-after was somehow attainable. Or at the very least, that a couple of good nights could be salvaged from the situation.

"Madison? You there?"

Out of the blue, a wave of nausea hit her. It ebbed, then flowed, just as it had with the motion of the boat. Maybe she just wasn't ready?

She was shaking her head before the words tumbled out of her mouth. "No, I don't think so, Blake. Goodbye."

She stared down at the phone in her hand, wondering what the heck just happened. For a woman who had been determined a few days ago that she needed a little fun in her life, this had been the most stressful attempt at fun she'd ever known.

It reminded her of her attempts throughout the years to carve out time for herself as a caregiver. She'd known she needed to renew her energy, to rest, but it had been too complicated to make it worth her while. By the time she'd hit on the one thing that brought her joy and was easy to fit into their lives, her father had fallen into a rapid decline. Death had followed not a month later.

A glance up showed a mixture of dismay and understanding on her friend's faces. Madison just continued to shake her head. "What the heck is wrong with me?"

Four

So Madison had forced him to move to plan C.

Blake couldn't believe it when Madison turned down his request for another date. What was he, the plague? She was nothing like any of the women he'd dated before, but he was realizing that that was part of what kept him intrigued.

He knew from being with her that Madison wasn't a typical woman, wealthy or otherwise. She'd had a very unique upbringing; she had an altruistic focus in her life. A unique woman called for a unique approach. Somehow he knew he wasn't giving her what she needed.

This was taking him a little while to figure out, because rejection was not his usual experience in life. It wasn't typical in his general daily dealings, in his business interactions and certainly not in his relationships. Not that he'd really call what he had *relationships*.

They were more like encounters, he realized.

Not one-night stands exactly, but his interactions with women rarely got too deep no matter how many times he saw them. He liked it that way. He kept it that way, because then he didn't have to deal with any ugly emotions or pain. The few tantrums or hissy fits he'd encountered had been surface-level, because the last thing he'd allowed was for any woman to get attached.

If there was one thing his father had inadvertently taught him, it was that the more you loved someone, the more they could hurt you.

Blake found a place to park his car, then got out and started to walk. To the casual onlooker, he was just strolling. Blake knew his destination, but he wasn't in any hurry to get there. He'd give Madison time to get settled in, and then he could show up. The edge of the Garden District at night was just as beautiful as it was during the day. The shadows of the stately homes created mystery and intrigue, showcasing a history that was barely hinted at in a casual glance. It was still early, but the heat had dissipated, allowing him to walk in relative comfort.

He was surprised he'd caught this little tidbit of Madison's life in the PI's notes. Though he'd read through the file his father had given him before, Madison's actions had sent him back to the drawing board. Another thorough read had shown him one line that he'd missed the first time around.

Sometime during the last year of her father's illness, Madison had managed to find herself a new side gig: singing. The little neighborhood pub was not too far from her house. As a matter of fact, it was within walking distance. She'd lucked out that it was so close, which had probably given her a chance to sneak away at night…maybe when her father was sleeping. There she spent a couple of hours creating atmosphere for those around her, and dreams for herself.

That little discovery had made having to reread the story of her sad upbringing worth it.

His father had been a big motivator, too. Surprise, surprise. After his continued refusal to let Blake see Abigail, Blake had confronted him to demand proof that she was okay. His father had once again refused, stating that Blake hadn't made any kind of progress that was worth rewarding him for.

He'd later called the housekeeper, who had loudly told him she could give him no updates, then whispered she was fine. But the ticking clock in his brain told him he had to do something soon, or else Abigail might not be there for him to see. He could only hope that Sherry would continue to keep an eye on her. He had a feeling that if time ran out, she'd either have a medical episode, or his father would end up sending her away.

Blake noticed his destination up ahead on the right. The little neighborhood hub was a hole in the wall that only locals would know about. The single door and dusty windows weren't enough to draw in tourists.

As Blake approached, he could smell a whiff of alcohol and a slight smokiness coming from the entrance, even though patrons were no longer allowed to smoke inside. He paused not far from the door, leaning against one of the support posts. A soft amber light glowed behind the milky windowpanes.

The voice hit him in a smooth, insistent way. He would have recognized it anywhere…but Madison's husky tone was enhanced somehow by the song. He closed his eyes and let the wave wash over him. The undertow was so smooth he would have willingly followed it anywhere. Suddenly Blake understood the stories he'd heard about sirens. He could feel himself falling under her spell; the words didn't even need to mean anything. It was simply a sound that filled empty parts of his soul he didn't even know he had.

In a moment of panic, his heart picked up speed. It felt as if something out of the ordinary was happening, and he might never be the same. Logically Blake scoffed at the idea. Still his heart and lungs continued to race.

"Incredible, isn't she?"

With a jerk, Blake realized he wasn't alone. In the dim light beneath the awning, he'd missed the grizzled bouncer seated on a stool on the opposite side of the doorway. His knee-length shorts, button-down shirt, leather vest and chest-length beard announced him as a biker all the way. His smile revealed a couple of broken teeth.

"Our Maddie is something else, right?" he asked again.

Blake nodded, still feeling a bit too unsteady to leave the support of the post. "Sure is," he said simply.

"The regulars love her, for good reason. I've heard a lot of talented voices in New Orleans, but hers is one of the best. Untrained, but still smooth as silk. She could tell you to go to hell and make you enjoy the ride."

Blake chuckled, then straightened up and paid the cover charge.

"Enjoy," the bouncer said.

Blake made his way through the tight quarters right inside the door. The bar was there on the left, the wood smooth and aged but still glossy. A couple of tables on the right were sparsely populated.

Several feet in, the room widened, opening into a much larger space with multiple tables. The crowd had gathered here to listen to Maddie sing.

Blake didn't bother with a table. Instead he slipped along the back wall and stood in the shadows to watch the sexy woman in the spotlight. She wore a simple blue dress that revealed curves he remembered from the first night he'd met her. She barely moved, yet somehow she gave the impression of keeping time with the music. Her gorgeous auburn waves were pulled up and back from her face, revealing the smooth column of her neck.

Once again the words of the song rolled over

him, tempting him to let his eyes drift closed so he could absorb every one. But he couldn't take his gaze from the woman on the stage. Her voice washed over him, luring him to stay, breaking through his barriers piece by piece.

"Can I get you a drink, hon?"

Blake realized he had indeed let his eyes drift shut. He glanced over at the waitress, whose expression was hard to make out in the dim light. He requested a whiskey, then turned back toward the stage, but the mood had been broken. He found himself a table and had a seat. The waitress delivered his drink. He sipped at it every couple minutes, letting the burn coat his throat.

Almost too soon Madison's set was done. He saw the waitress whisper to her and nod in his direction. He wasn't sure how she'd known he was here for her, but even from across the bar he could see the flush that stained Madison's cheeks.

She should be used to men being drawn in by her voice, so was the blush for him in particular?

She approached and slid into the seat across from him.

"Drink?" he asked.

She shook her head, and something inside him became impatient. The urge to hear her speak, to compare that voice to the one he'd heard from the stage, grew as the seconds slid by.

But when she did speak, her voice came out hard. "What are you doing here? You aren't supposed to be here. No one is supposed to know—"

He leaned back in his chair. This wasn't at all what he'd expected. "I'm just glad I did."

"I'm not."

Blake frowned, surprised by the pushback. "Why?"

She drew in a deep breath, glancing around as she slowly released it. "I've just never shared this with anyone before. It's private."

Blake perused the people filling the small bar. But it was the room itself that helped him understand her protest. The stage was lit with a spotlight, but the rest of the room was cast in dusky shadow. Here Madison could have her own space, indulge in something she loved, practically anonymously, and be free of her burdens for a few hours.

"I know it doesn't make sense—"

"No, Madison. It's okay. I'm sorry for intruding."

She swallowed and dropped her gaze to the table-top. "Why are you here?" she whispered, barely loud enough for him to catch it over the people speaking now that the music had ended.

"I've never explored much of New Orleans, so I decided to take a walk and happened by." Which sounded lame, even to him. "I got drawn right in. Your voice is incredible, Madison." *There you go. Distract her with the partial truth.* "I feel privileged to have heard you sing."

"No. Why are you here with me?" She patted the table with her palms in emphasis. "Why are you even interested in me?"

"Madison…" He wasn't sure what to say. The answer to that became more complicated with every minute he sat here.

"You shouldn't be. I'm not like them."

"Who?"

"The women in the pictures. I saw them online." She shook her head. "I'm not like them. I'm broke and awkward and a caretaker and have obligations. I'm just not a casual kind of person, Blake. I want to be...but I don't know how."

Every word rang in his head, confirming why he was here. She wasn't anything like what he was used to—and he liked that. The fact that her assumptions about him were so close to what he was like any other day made him angry. At himself, for being so shallow. At her, for buying into his public image.

True panic sizzled up until it popped like a champagne cork. "Damn it. Don't you think I know that, Madison? With all those women, nothing about them kept me coming back. But I can't stop coming back to you. Do you even understand what that means?"

Where had that come from? They stared at one another in silence. Blake breathed hard, his mind racing. His brain replayed the words he'd said, words he wished he could take back. It was a truth he hadn't wanted to face...much less blurt out to Madison like that.

But he couldn't take it back...so he waited.

His heart pounded as he kept waiting for her answer. As much as he wanted to convince himself that his nerves hinged on Abigail's fate, that it was about his father's demands, deep down he knew he'd just made it something more. Something personal.

Was that why this felt more real than anything he'd ever experienced before?

Then she spoke. "For something that was supposed to be *just fun,* this has sure gotten complicated."

Her words, so closely echoing his own thoughts, startled him. He quickly hid his reaction and asked, "What do you mean?"

"I don't understand why a guy like you is here with me. You're champagne and caviar. I'm—" she waved her hand "—just not."

"Maybe we need to explore that difference. No obligations."

This was it. This was the key he'd been looking for. So why wasn't he elated? Instead, anticipation and fear sizzled in his veins. "So what do you say?"

"I still don't understand."

He didn't want her to. The truth would be devastating—maybe to both of them.

"But yes," she conceded.

He lifted his glass in a toast, and was relieved when she nodded her consent. The burn centered him once more. He set his glass on the table, rimming the edge with his index finger. He needed this conversation back on a smoother track. "So I guess a hot-air balloon ride is out, right?"

Madison laughed, pressing the palm of her hand against her stomach. "Let's not risk it." She studied him for a moment. "So you haven't seen much of New Orleans? Not even as a kid?"

"No." The pressure of her gaze urged him to elaborate, but for once he kept quiet. His childhood was something he never wanted to relive, even in memories.

"Well, how about I show you my version?"

"Are you sure you want to walk?" Blake asked as he met her on a corner of the outer edge of the Garden District a few nights later. "I'm happy to drive."

"Don't be a baby. It's barely even summer here," Madison teased.

Besides, the June heat was starting to dissipate as evening fell on the Garden District. The only way to get a good feel for this town was to walk it.

"You can't experience the essence of New Orleans in a vehicle," she said, "unless it's a streetcar."

"Those are just tourist traps," Blake scoffed, but he fell into step beside her.

"Those are history," Madison corrected. "And a lot of people use them besides tourists."

"God forbid."

Madison paused to study him, one brow lifted. Blake either hadn't been exposed to the history of New Orleans, as he'd admitted, or he made a habit of not looking at a place too closely. "Just for that, I'm going to make you ride one. A lot of people commute on those things."

"I'm not sure I'd fit in with my designer shoes." He struck a pose, a grin forming on his too-perfect face. His words and actions were a reminder to keep things casual. A reminder she definitely needed.

How was she supposed to manage that?

"Pretty spiffy," she agreed, keeping her tone light, "but you'll be fine. I'm starting to get the feeling you didn't really see all these countries you claim to have visited. Not really."

He shrugged. "Maybe not." But the line that appeared between his brows told her he didn't feel as casual as he let on.

She didn't want to ask what he'd really been doing in them. All those pictures of him with supermodel types told her most of what she didn't want to know. Instead, she resumed her stroll along the sidewalk. As they walked, the tall, stately houses gave way to smaller, crowded buildings that contained businesses.

As they paused on one corner, a bus stopped at the red light. Its door opened and the older man called from the driver's seat, "Hey, Madison."

"Hi, Frankie," she hollered back. "How did your granddaughter's soccer game go?"

"She scored the winning goal," he answered with a toothy grin and a thumbs-up before heading on down the road.

Not too much farther along, ol' Mr. Paddington rounded the corner, walking his golden retriever. Madison paused to say good evening and pat the dog's head as she passed.

At Blake's curious look, she said, "Mr. Paddington lost his wife recently to a stroke. I encouraged him to get the dog to give him something to do. He walks her every evening about this time."

A couple more blocks down, an elderly woman in a floral housedress paused while sweeping her front porch to wave. "Evening, Madison," she yelled.

Madison raised her hand in greeting but didn't stop this time. Maybe this hadn't been the best route. She hadn't thought about how many interruptions they might run into.

They crossed another street to a corner, where a familiar gentleman sat on a stool in the shade. His lovely saxophone blended with the sounds of traffic and commerce around them, and had for more years than Madison could count. She dropped a couple of coins in the open case at his feet. "Night, Bartholomew."

"Thanks, Miss Madison," he said.

They strolled along in silence for a few minutes before Blake glanced over at her. "Is there anyone you don't know around here?"

"I've been walking this area since I was a kid. So honestly, not many. We lost a lot of people during Katrina and afterward, but new ones have moved in and that's been a blessing."

The sights and scents around her drew her in, enveloping her in a cozy feeling that had nothing to do with the fading heat of the day. She nodded at a small bakery, then a hometown pizza restaurant across the street. "All these places have been here for years. My mama used to walk up here when she was busy taking care of my dad. One of the special adventures she would take me on when I was a little kid was to get a free cookie from that bakery. They gave one to every kid who came in the door, and sometimes they'd be nice and give me two. I'd always share with my mama. I think the owner knew that.

"After her death, it was my turn to take care of my daddy." Madison pressed her lips together for a minute. Was she revealing too much?

"What was wrong with him?"

"Multiple sclerosis. At first he thought he was in a severe depression after losing his business in a bankruptcy, but he progressively got worse. You never knew what a day would bring with him. My mother died when I was sixteen. This was the extent of her world, and mine for a long time." She didn't mention that they'd rarely had money for her to go anywhere else. Abruptly Madison paused, realizing just how much she'd said.

She'd intended to introduce Blake to her New Orleans…not spill the details of her sad and meager childhood. The sounds of the cars on the road and music coming from the stores covered their silence for several steps while she tried to figure out how to keep this conversation from getting too deep.

"Speaking of houses, when are you going to invite me over?"

Apparently Blake didn't have the same issues about boundaries. Or most likely, he had no idea what a touchy subject her home had become.

Having him over was the last thing Madison wanted to do. *So much for a modern girl's attitude…* As much as she hated how shallow it sounded, Blake was loaded. Money was not something Madison had ever had. Only now was she able to truly make a living with her job at Maison de Jardin.

The house that had once been a showplace of the area now had overgrown hedges to block the sight of it from the road. The disrepair from years of having to make do with a shoestring budget was something that embarrassed her greatly. She'd done what she could to keep up with the major fixes, but the broken windows, peeling paint, warped flooring and the lack of a new roof were sore issues for her right now.

The very knowledge that she would soon need to sell off her family home made her heart ache, but she knew it was for the best. It was taking every bit of her current salary to get it up to snuff. There was no way she could maintain the house in the glory it deserved.

A lot of people bought houses in the Garden District specifically to renovate them, and she was hoping her house would be lucky enough to have the same fate. Soon, but not yet.

"Are you staying far from here?" she asked, hoping to distract him.

He went along with it for now. "I'm in an apartment in the business district, but my family lives on one of the old plantations."

Madison smiled, taken back to her vivid daydreams of open spaces and old barns as a child. "I bet that was a magical place to grow up."

"It was a hell with no means of escape." A brief glance showed her a fake grin on Blake's face to go with his harsh tone. "But then childhood memories are often exaggerated in our minds, right?"

She wasn't so sure. Memories of the hard years of her childhood had softened with age, but they never went away. She reminded herself that that wasn't why they were here tonight; this was about fun, not digging deep. Luckily, the place she had planned for dinner was just ahead. That should steer the conversation in another direction.

They stepped through the door with its peeling paint and a jingle bell over it into a long, narrow galley kitchen.

"Madison!" An African American woman rushed from behind the counter to hug her. Bebe was old enough to be her grandmother but appeared timeless with her smooth, dark skin. "It's so good to see you. And who's your friend?"

"Bebe, this is Blake. And I told him he needed to have the best po'boy in the city of New Orleans for dinner."

Blake gave the dim conditions of the room the side-eye but seemed to be won over by the woman's smile.

Bebe's grin was contagious, as always. She pulled off her apron to give Madison a hug. "Girl, you are skin and bones. You need a po'boy and then some."

Madison just smiled. "All that mothering instinct coming to the fore."

"Yes, ma'am." Bebe's smile turned down at the edges. "And I'm happy to report Talia is doing better."

Madison gave her friend a little extra squeeze before turning her loose.

Bebe glanced over at Blake. "Love this one like a daughter. She's the same age as my own Talia, whose undergoing cancer treatments right now." She patted Madison's arm while Madison blinked back tears. "This girl can make me smile on the worst of days."

Then Bebe went back behind the counter. As soon as she put her apron back on it was all business. "What can I make you?"

Madison's throat had closed up so that speaking was impossible. Blake stepped up to the counter. "How about Maddie's favorite…times two?"

Bebe beamed her approval and got to work. Soon she handed the food back over the counter, then leaned over to give Madison a kiss on her cheek. "You have a good evening, darling," she said as they headed out the door with their heavy bag.

"This way," Madison said.

A couple of stores down, a narrow alleyway opened to the right. She led him down the space barely wide enough for his shoulders. As they walked, she took a few more deep breaths to try to clear her emotions away. Seeing Bebe was always a mix of happy and sad, but that was how they got through the tough times. Madison just hadn't thought about it before taking him in there. She'd just wanted to show him some of her favorite places.

Finally they reached the end of the alley to face a black wrought iron fence. Taking a few steps to the side, Madison reached for the latch to let them in. And this was her favorite place of all.

"What is this?" Blake asked as they stepped into a lush, overgrown garden.

The centerpiece was a beautiful cherry tree, surrounded by various ferns, hostas and an abundance of moss growing in the shade. Tucked into one corner was a small wrought iron table and chairs.

"This is one of my favorite places in the whole city," she said. "The garden is actually part of the St. Andrew's Catholic Church. My mother brought me here as a child, and we would eat our cookies while enjoying the cool and quiet."

She noticed Blake cock his head to the side like he was listening for something. Sure enough, the buildings and lush foliage blocked out the sound of the busy street not too far away. Despite living in the city, Madison had a deep love of nature and enjoyed these green spaces. Being here gave her a sense of peace and calm that everyday life seemed to withhold. But wasn't that the same for everybody?

Maybe not, but she'd take peace where she could get it. Even now her heart rate was slowing and those unwelcome tears were seeping away.

"The priests don't mind because they knew we would never leave a mess. The church allowed my mother's services here when she died."

"This is beautiful," he said simply.

"You should see the conservatory at Maison de Jardin. It's absolutely gorgeous."

She started to unpack their dinner, needing a distraction from the minefield of memories. How come she couldn't just have fun?

"How did you go to work there?" Blake asked as they settled in. "You're very young to be the director of that large a charity."

In years, maybe. She didn't want to talk about the experience that had made her qualified for her job. "Trinity, the former director, has known me for a long time. Knows what I'm capable of. But she's still very hands-on."

She paused to take a bite of the sandwich, enjoying the resistance of the bread and the crunch of the fried crawfish. "What do you do?"

He immediately popped off, "According to my father, nothing."

Whoa.

Blake jumped to his feet and paced in the small space. Madison held really still. Should she say something? This went way beyond their surface chatter tonight. Not that she'd stuck to her goal of keeping it light very well herself.

He was quiet for so long the back of her neck tightened. Was he looking for a way to blow the statement off? Then she realized she didn't know enough about Blake to counteract his bitter statement in any way. Just as panic set in, he turned back toward her and leaned against the tree trunk behind him.

"Is he right?" she asked, blowing off all of her angst and going with her instincts.

"Partly." He offered a half smile. "But less than he knows."

A lightbulb went off. "Your drawings?"

"How did you—of course, you noticed. You see a lot, don't you?"

"Is that a good thing?"

"Probably not." He pushed away from the tree and crossed to her side. "Definitely not."

Before Madison could blink, Blake had her in his arms, his lips barely meeting hers. But he didn't rush. He waited for her to open, granting him permission to press forward. Then he sampled, testing and tasting her lips in smooth, slow strokes. Madison's spine lit up. The spicy taste of him on her tongue left her ravenous for way more than food.

After long moments he pulled back, leaving her dazed and a little unsteady on her feet. She opened her eyes, blinking once or twice before focusing in on the golden, angular lines of his face. Only to see them softened by his smile as he said, "I'm not comfortable with you seeing things, but I think it's more than worth it."

Five

Blake dove back in for another taste, leaving Madison breathless and gasping. The feel of him intoxicated her. She had the resistance of a rag doll as he pulled her into his lap. More naturally than she would have imagined, she found herself straddling his thighs. Belly to belly. Face to face.

As his mouth traveled from her lips, over her jaw, to her neck, she struggled to pull air into her lungs. The excitement of his touch, the racing of her pulse, the need to press herself closer to him despite the heat in the air…how was this happening?

Something tickled the back of her mind, something she should remember, but nothing intruded on the sensations evoked by the man beneath her. She clutched at his shoulders, kneading the well-defined muscles, not sure whether she was trying to steady herself or imprint him with her touch. A fire rose inside her, forcing her to squirm, needing relief from the intense sensations pooling low in her belly.

Madison rocked forward. Blake gasped against her skin, his hands squeezing her arms. "Madison," he groaned.

Her pulse pounded at the base of her throat. After one last hot, openmouthed kiss, he pulled back. "We have to stop. Right now."

"Why?" she whispered. She should know the answer, but right now it was as far from her as possible.

"We have to," he said. He rested his forehead against her collarbone, breathing heavy in the hush of the garden. "I had no idea how addictive you would be."

Well, no one had ever called her that. She drew in a deep breath, searching for equilibrium. How had this gotten so out of hand?

"May I help you?" a voice asked from the shadows.

Madison started, realizing they weren't alone. Instinctively she jerked back, and lost her balance because she was on Blake's lap. With a cry, she fell, landing on her backside on one of the stone pavers surrounding the table. She ignored the pain. Instead she focused in on the source of the voice. "Father Stephen… I'm so sorry."

The younger of the priests here—at forty-five—gave her a soft smile. "I see that."

Blake reached out and helped Madison to her feet. "Honestly, Father," he added. "I apologize for—"

He broke off and a flush of red tinged the skin right above his magnificent cheekbones. Madison would have giggled if she wasn't aware that her entire face was on fire, too.

"Yes, well, maybe it's time to finish your dinner? Yes, Madison?" the man asked.

Madison guessed it was a good thing he knew her, or else she'd probably have been arrested for... something. But that thought made her embarrassment burn even hotter. "Yes, sir. I'll—we'll do that."

"See that you do," he said. "And I'll see you at mass Saturday night."

Madison choked on her emotions as the man retreated around the corner to the back door of the church. She only dared to glance over at Blake when he chuckled. He shook his head as he said, "Well, that was embarrassing."

"He hasn't known you since you were a baby. Imagine how I feel."

Blake held out her chair for her to sit back down at the table. "Oh, I don't have to imagine."

The suggestive comment should have put her back up. Instead, she covered her face with her hands and let laughter release her tension. Now that her head had cleared somewhat from the kiss, she could finally put her finger on what had been bothering her...they were in public.

It was the first time she'd ever managed to forget that...

Blake simply picked up his sandwich and continued to eat.

"How can you—" Men were obviously very different from women. Or maybe it was just her and her lack of experience with these things.

She simply stared at him until he met her gaze once more. It made her feel a little better when his smile had a sheepish tinge. "Well, I'm not about to let a little embarrassment keep me away from the rest of this po'boy. You weren't wrong about it being the best in New Orleans."

She recognized his attempt to return things to normal, and did her best to relax. "I hope you mean that, because I eat at Bebe's all the time."

"I'm on board for that."

They ate in silence for a few minutes. Madison preferred not to think about the last few minutes. Maybe later tonight, alone in her room, she would. But if she thought about it now, she'd never be able to carry on a conversation. Instead she cast her mind back to what they'd been discussing before.

"I'm sorry that your father can't see the value in your art," she said.

As hard as her life had been, Madison's father had always made his appreciation plain. He'd hated what she had to do to keep them afloat, but he'd always expressed gratitude for her hard work and dedication.

"My father is not an easy man." Blake's smile wasn't as convincing as he probably wanted. "And I would have said that was no longer an issue for me. But, well, family is never easy."

Instantly the picture he'd drawn that first night came to mind. "So you draw for a living?"

He shrugged. "I wouldn't necessarily call it a living. I had a lot of help from my inheritance from my mother, which would have let me live a careful existence without working for the rest of my life. But I'm rarely careful…"

"But you are a very talented artist." Even in her inexperience, she could see that.

"Some people think so, and they are willing to pay for my drawings." He glanced away, studying the lush foliage around them for long moments. "That was a very complicated answer to an easy question."

"Sometimes the easy answer isn't the best." She couldn't keep the words from slipping out. "I'm sorry, Blake."

He studied her for a moment. "Why?"

She shook her head. "I tried to keep whatever this is between us on the surface, just fun, but everything about tonight has run completely counter to that. I don't feel comfortable, like I'm lying to you. This just…isn't me." Her smile was sad, apologetic. "I realize that now. And I'm sorry. I know that's not what you want."

"Are you sure?"

They both seemed equally surprised by the question. Then he cocked up one blond brow. "Quite frankly, I'm willing to hang around until we find out what it *is*. Not what it *should* be."

"Really?"

He winked at her. "Really."

That should be a good thing…so why was she shaking over the prospect?

* * *

"Let me see Abigail. Now."

Blake's father offered him a smile that had nothing to do with being happy. "Slow down," he cautioned. "You didn't seem to be making any progress the last time you checked in. Did you bring me some proof?"

For a moment, Blake just stared in disbelief. Arguing the way he wanted to would probably get him nowhere.

"What kind of proof are you looking for?"

"A pair of panties?"

Gross. Why would he—? "I don't have to sleep with Madison to get the diamond."

"But you do have to spend time with her, and get invited into her house. Which as far as I can tell, hasn't happened, either…"

His father's straight back and braced arms told Blake he wasn't backing down. So instead of saying more, Blake pulled out his phone and offered up a picture of him and Madison together in the garden at the church. His father nodded slowly as he studied it.

"Not the most efficient method in my book, but good job."

Those words grated over every nerve, forcing Blake to clench his teeth. His father had often told him "good job" as a child, usually after berating him for making a choice he wouldn't have, then forcing Blake to do things his way.

His father leaned closer, staring at the phone. Blake was surprised to see his lips tighten. "Let me guess," he finally said, his tone now clipped. "The garden behind St. Andrew's?"

Blake nodded slowly. "How did you know?" After all, he couldn't imagine his father being anywhere near that part of town.

"Her mother and I met there a couple of times."

Whoa. That wasn't what Blake had expected.

Then again, he couldn't imagine his father meeting a woman anywhere other than at a fancy party. There he could easily disguise his narcissistic attitude with fancy clothes and jewelry. Polite small talk. And offers of fancy outings.

That brought Blake up short. Wasn't that exactly what he had tried to offer Madison? To impress her? To keep things polite and on a superficial level?

Well, that approach hadn't lasted with this particular woman, had it? All it had taken was one physical touch to shake him. Madison's response hadn't been practiced or lukewarm. It had been real, full-bodied passion.

And Blake had found it amazing.

His father and a woman anything like Madison? He just couldn't imagine it. "Why are you doing this? Her mother is dead. Revenge is going to accomplish nothing."

Familiar rage seemed to make his father grow larger and more menacing. At least this time Blake was too big to be intimidated. "She should have been mine," he growled as he strode across the tile floor, his dress shoes clicking as he moved.

"And since you couldn't possess her, you now

have to take back what didn't belong to you? After all these years? Come on… I'm not buying that."

He stopped abruptly. "Desperate times call for desperate measures."

"You're never desperate," Blake argued. "Cold. Calculating. But not desperate."

"In this economy, everyone is desperate."

"Money?" He should have known. But his father had always been more than solvent. What had gone wrong?

"Isn't it always about money?"

"No. Usually it's about people." Even when it seemed to be about money, for people like Madison, that money was necessary for keeping her family fed, housed, clothed. Not for fancy cars and travel.

"I made a few bad investments," his father said with a too casual shrug. "With that diamond, I'll be set."

"But it doesn't belong to you."

"I'll take whatever I have to. I did before, and I will continue to as long as necessary."

Suspicion filtered through Blake's consciousness. "Father? I know that tone. You couldn't have had anything to do with her father's illness. And I certainly hope you had nothing to do with her mother's death. What's the deal?" he demanded.

His father brushed at a nonexistent spot on his jacket. "No, unfortunately those issues were beyond me. But I made sure they didn't have the money to do much about them, now, didn't I? I set out to ruin

Jacqueline's husband, and that was one goal I managed to accomplish."

Blake held silent. So this steady downward spiral of Madison's father's business, the bankruptcy that killed his spirit, had been his own father's fault? Why wasn't he surprised?

"So your only plan for pulling yourself out of the red is to steal from a young woman who deserves no punishment whatsoever?"

"She'll never miss what she's never had."

Blake should be surprised, but even after all these years, he remembered that the only person his father cared about was himself. If his finances were in that dire a state, he wouldn't hesitate to strike out, no matter who it was. If it wasn't Madison, it might just be Abigail.

His father turned away, cutting the conversation off. "I guess you deserve a little reward, for what progress you've made. Just make it quick. Abigail might be in her room. She's as slippery as you were when you were a kid. Always where she doesn't belong."

Blake heard the patter of tiny feet as he stepped onto the first stair in the foyer. He moved slower than he should have, considering the concern that had built over the last week. What did he know about talking to a child?

The few times he'd been with Abigail before, her mother and nanny had been present. She'd been cute and engaging, but children were completely out of Blake's league. He moved down the hallway to an open door and glanced inside. The pale pink walls, frilly pictures and a large silver monogram of the girl's initials hanging over the headboard showed that her mother had at least decorated before she left. Abigail sat in a puddle of fluffy blankets on the bed. The dim light in the room didn't reveal much about her, so he reached out to flick on the light switch.

She blinked in the extra brightness.

Those big brown eyes, so reminiscent of her mother's, made her look vulnerable in a way Blake wasn't comfortable with.

What should he say after not seeing her for two years? "How are you, Abigail?" he asked. Lame, but he had to start somewhere.

She shrugged, but Blake remembered that response from his own childhood. He wasn't going to be brushed off.

"Tell me, Abigail." He made sure their gazes met. "I really want to know. Miss Sherry said you'd been sick."

"Those pills make me feel tired."

Was that normal? Blake wasn't even sure whom he would ask.

"But my head doesn't feel funny anymore."

So maybe the medicine was working? Her color looked healthy. Could you tell anything about epilepsy from just watching her? He needed to investigate that more.

"I'm sorry," she whispered.

Distracted from his obsessive worrying, he came closer and sat beside the bed. "Why are you sorry?"

"If I hadn't gotten sick, none of this would've happened."

Blake's heart sank. No child should have to feel responsible for the actions of the adults around them. Blake should not have had to feel responsible for his father's anger, for his mother's incompetence, for the string of stepmothers who moved in and out of his life. "Abigail," he said, searching for the right words. "You don't have to be sorry. Scratch that. You should not be sorry. None of this is your fault."

"But Mommy left me."

"And that's her fault." Blake didn't bring up the fact that her mother simply wasn't strong enough to handle anything outside of his father. He didn't want her more fearful that she already was. "You being sick, it just…is."

"Why?"

"I'm not sure." Man, saying that made him feel inadequate. He was probably screwing this up royally, but he didn't know how else to proceed. "I have to go, but if you need me, you just need to tell Miss Sherry to call me, okay?" The housekeeper had given him frequent updates, even though they'd been short to avoid detection from her boss.

Abigail nodded slowly. The move was solemn enough to make Blake's chest ache. "Look, I don't know when he'll let me come back. But I want you to remember, I *will* be back."

Her deep brown eyes filled with tears, but she blinked them back in an all too familiar move. Blake remembered that vividly from a time or two during his childhood. "Promise?"

"Promise." Even if he had to walk over hot coals. Which would actually be preferable to complying with his father's demands.

Six

Madison took a deep breath, trying to calm the nerves in her stomach.

She always had butterflies at the beginning of a performance, but this was different. This was her first time knowing she was singing in front of Blake. The first time she wasn't craving that chance to close her eyes and lose herself in a different world.

Normally when she was up here on stage, she didn't see the crowd. She didn't hear the clapping. She didn't pay attention to any hecklers. She lost herself in an inner world of melody mixed with darkness. A place where she felt happy and safe.

Tonight she felt the glare of the spotlight. But she needed it, wanted it. She could no longer deny that she wanted to see where this thing between her and

Blake would go. The only way to find out was to dive in deep, and stop questioning every single stroke.

And he'd given her the perfect opportunity by showing up tonight.

Madison caught her cue and opened her mouth to sing. Tonight, instead of losing herself in the darkness, she sang for Blake alone. Every rhythm, every note was for him. As if they were alone in the room.

She braced her heels against the wooden planks of the stage. The mic stand felt cool between her palms.

She couldn't see him, but she could feel him. Feel his gaze as it roamed every inch of the silky green dress she wore. Her blood raced through her veins, as if the very act of singing were foreplay. She was amazed at how good this felt…and at her ability to let go and embrace what she realized she wanted.

A real relationship. Yes, she wanted it to be fun. But she wasn't capable of living on the surface. And if he was okay with it being more, then they'd see where this would go.

If it ended, it would hurt more. But Madison's life had been a series of endings, and she knew she'd survive.

This time when her set was over, she met Blake at his table with a drink of her own and slid into the seat opposite him as if they were strangers. The glass between her hands steadied her. "What brings you here?" she asked with what she hoped was a sexy smile.

His half smile sped up her heartbeat. "I heard there was a very sexy singer that I just had to see."

"I hope she didn't disappoint."

"Never," he said, his tone dropping an octave.

Even in the dark she could see his gaze dip down to the V-neckline of her dress, tracing the arrow down to her cleavage. Secretly she'd wanted to show off and had chosen this dress for that very purpose. Hoping he'd be here. Hoping he'd want more.

It looked like her hope just might turn into reality.

"You look beautiful tonight, Madison."

"You're not so bad yourself, Blake."

"How late will you be—"

A gravelly male voice interrupted. "Well, I should've known you'd be here, sugar."

Blake looked up, but Madison kept her gaze trained on him. Her teeth clenched.

She recognized the voice. One she'd dreaded hearing ever since her daddy had died. The man was a nuisance at best. His visits to their house had always upset her father. As an adult, she'd realized the man had been trying to buy the house out from under them. But he'd never wanted to pay a decent price for it. Or maybe her daddy had been like her. It really didn't matter who the house went to, as long as it didn't go to this obnoxious, self-entitled boob.

Finally Maddie looked away from Blake's enticing blue eyes up at the man's face. His overtanned skin and calculating look repulsed her. "Hello, John Mark. How are you?"

Not that she really wanted to know, but it was polite to ask.

The middle-aged, heavyset man pulled over a

chair from another table and turned it around backward so he could straddle it. He held out his hand to Blake. "Hi there, I'm John Mark. I don't think we've been introduced."

"I don't guess so," Blake said, glancing back and forth between the two of them.

Madison had been raised to have manners, to be accommodating of other people even when you didn't care for them. But somehow she couldn't summon it tonight. Her greeting had used up her store of politeness. She could feel a frown pulling down the edges of her mouth and eyebrows. The energy to lift them just was beyond her. This man was associated with so many irritating memories from when her father was alive, and that gloom settled over her like a weighted blanket.

She didn't bother to contribute to the expected introductions. Hopefully the dim lighting would hide the animosity in her expression.

"I don't think I've ever seen you in here, John Mark," she said instead. That was one good reason to keep coming to the club. It had always felt like her safe place. What was with the sudden invasion?

"Oh, but I knew you would be here," he said. "And it's long past time we talk some business."

"I don't really think this is the time or place—"

"Of course it is," he said with a grin that was too wide. "Besides, you're a hard woman to catch. Always here or there. And nobody's returning calls from the house. In the meantime, that place is gonna fall down around your ears."

Blake cleared his throat. "I don't really think…"

"Oh, she knows what I'm after," John Mark replied with a careless wave of his hand. "I begged her father to sell me that house for years. Now it's time."

The audacity of his words hit Madison the wrong way. Heated pressure grew deep inside her. "Actually, I don't think there's anything for us to talk about."

John Mark wasn't listening. "I will take that house off your hands real easy, young lady. You just sign over the paperwork and the headache is no longer yours."

Madison knew she needed to sell the house, but not to this man. *Never* this man. "The house isn't ready…"

"There's no need to do anything to it. I'm pretty sure I know how bad a shape it's in. I might have to tear it down and start over, but that's a prime piece of land. It's a shame your daddy let it get that bad, but he wouldn't get out when his body gave up on him, would he?"

Madison felt the tips of her ears start to burn. The pressure rose, mixing with grief for her father and anger over this man's casual words. The last thing she wanted was for Blake to find out the true state of affairs with her family like this.

"When I am ready, I'll—"

"You'll never be ready. Just sign the papers."

"No." The pressure erupted. "And do not talk over me."

Madison stood, feeling more in control on her feet. She wasn't sure where the steel in her voice came from, but she wasn't being railroaded into any-thing she didn't want to do. "Do not come to my house. Do not call on the phone. I'm not selling my place to you. Ever."

John Mark glanced back and forth between them, a smile spreading across his face. "Now, there's no need to get into a tizzy, little lady."

"Ev-ver."

Something in her face or tone must've finally told him she was serious. His thin lips pressed together, a scowl curving his brows. "Beggars aren't in a po-sition to be choosers. Don't be stupid."

"Back off," Blake said, a growl underlying his tone.

"Why? She's not going to get a better offer. And she desperately needs one… I could tell that with one glance around that place. I always did wonder how you kept it up." He gave Blake the once-over, clearly taking in his fancy watch. "Guess now I know, huh?"

Instantly Blake was on his feet, crowding John Mark away from the table. There was a flurry of ac-tivity as the bouncer headed their way, and a low ex-change of voices between the men that she couldn't quite catch. But Blake's advantage in height seemed to make an impression on the bulky man. He raised his hands in surrender.

The bouncer grabbed John Mark's arm. "This guy bothering you, Miss Maddie?"

At first she just nodded, not trusting her voice. As John Mark started to protest, she stepped in close. "My daddy was always a good judge of character.

He had you pegged as slimy from the beginning. I do believe I agree." She nodded at the bouncer, who strong-armed him away.

For a moment, Madison stood still, stunned at what had happened, until Blake led her back over to the table. "Are you okay?"

Madison melted into the seat, the starch in her spine washing away. "I just can't catch a break. Every time I'm around you something stupid happens." She plopped back in her seat, trying hard not to let the tears well up. That would just be the icing on the cake.

"It's not stupid. You have no control over him showing up," Blake insisted.

"But why did it have to happen right now, right in the middle of—"

"It's okay, Madison."

She smacked her palm against the table, her voice rising. "It's not okay. I didn't want you to find out about that."

Blake tilted his head to the side in question.

"On the good days, I can handle the fact that I'm going to have to sell my family home. I've done the best that I can. My father did the best that he could. And I know it has to go. That's the way it is, but that doesn't make it hurt any less."

She stared down into her drink. For a moment, she was at a total loss. Her normal go-to was to get up and do something to fix it. And there was no fixing this.

She could walk away, and leave Blake sitting here

by himself. She could hang around and let him convince her that it was all okay. He didn't need to—she knew her own worth. The state of her house embarrassed her, but considering the state of their finances when she was growing up, she knew she had done the best that she could. And if Blake couldn't understand that, then she needed to walk away.

Or she could do what her body and soul had been telling her since she'd met him. She could walk toward him, and let happen whatever happened. Accept his decisions and make the memories she wanted so badly.

She glanced back at him and saw his blue eyes trained steadily on her. No hint of embarrassment, no signs of anger or irritation. Just watching her. Maybe he was looking for the next clue?

Just then the waitress interrupted, drawing Maddie's attention to her with a hand on her shoulder. "Hon, are you going to finish the night out?"

Normally Madison would never walk away from her gig under any circumstances, but tonight she simply couldn't continue. "No, I need to go home."

The waitress squeezed her shoulder before walking away. It was wonderful to work with people who were so understanding.

With a pounding heart, she glanced back over at Blake. "Would you like to go with me?"

Blake stared up at the house as he turned off his car. The silence that surrounded them had almost an echo to it, as if there were unspoken words surrounding them. The history of the place, maybe? Blake wasn't sure, and he was hesitant to look too deeply.

This was what he'd wanted all along. To be inside this house, to be given an opportunity to search through it. Hell, he'd even prepared himself for a one-night stand in order to do it.

But what he was walking into tonight wasn't a one-night stand. He was walking through those doors in an emotional state that he'd never anticipated. Because Maddie was real; she was more real to him than any woman he'd slept with before. And he had a feeling there would be no going back after tonight.

"Everything okay?" she asked.

He could hear the slight tremble in her voice. She was nervous. Blake knew that she was opening herself up in a way that she wouldn't ever have with someone else. That vulnerability, that choice humbled him.

He tried to remind himself about Abigail. He tried to remember his purpose, but all he could think about was Maddie. He glanced over at her in the dark. "Yes," he lied. "I'm fine."

Blake let himself out of the car and crossed around to her side to open the door. The driveway was tight, crowded on each side with an overgrowth of bushes. The oddly planted tree here or there. Was the overgrowth on purpose? Or simply one of those things that hadn't registered in the list of tasks that Madison faced every day?

He gave her just enough room to slip out the door, then closed it behind her. He pressed in close, trapping her between the vehicle and the hardness of his body. "Madison," he whispered, in deference to the quiet surrounding them. "I want you to remember something."

He could feel the shiver that went through her, and knew it had nothing to do with the temperature. The heated night closed in on them, but still her body responded. "Yes?"

That deep huskiness in her murmur shot straight down his spine. "Just remember, I want to be here."

Those simple words felt like more of a commitment than he could ever have imagined. Then he turned quickly toward the house, catching her hand in his.

Madison led him around the back and put her key in the door. The bushes surrounding the house were also out of control, some of them flowering crape myrtles, some overgrown hydrangeas. The heavy scent of flowers on the night air was intoxicating.

The door opened smoothly, to his surprise. A small mudroom opened up into a large kitchen. It was obvious that a lot of time was spent here. It gleamed with scrubbing. A meticulously maintained work surface that could possibly be original to the house gave the room a warm feeling that Blake could honestly say he'd never experienced in any house he'd lived in.

It wasn't until they moved on to other rooms that the wear and tear begin to make itself known. Bits of peeling paint. Cracked floor tile. Dim lighting where the bulbs in the chandeliers were obviously blown. Some rooms were closed off completely.

Madison kept her head down, as if she could ignore the signs of age if she didn't get a close enough look. Moving through the foyer, she did an abrupt turn to go up the stairs. Through the open doorway on the opposite side, Blake caught a glance of multiple pieces of furniture in various states of repair.

"What's this?" he asked, leaning into the doorway.

Madison paused about a quarter of the way up the stairs and looked back down at him. Her reluctance to return was clear, even in the shadows. After a moment's pause, she slowly came down one step at a time before reaching his side.

"What's this?" he asked again, not acknowledging her hesitation.

She stood next to him in the doorway but didn't glance into the room. "It's just a hobby," she said in a rush.

"It's a pretty expensive hobby…" The room had to contain at least ten pieces of furniture that were being refurbished. "That's a lot of elbow grease."

He glanced to the side to see Madison's arms crossed tightly over her rib cage. Apparently he'd waded into another touchy subject. But he really did want to know. This was obviously important to her, which spoke to him on a level he'd never experienced with other women.

"Come on, Maddie," he coaxed. "Tell me the truth."

She shot a quick glance up at him, her pupils wide and searching.

Finally she said, "John Mark wasn't wrong when he said times were tough. My father used to be a very affluent businessman, before he married my mama. But something…went wrong. He never would say what. They lost most of what they had. She did her best, and kept things fairly on track. But after she died, he just couldn't keep it together anymore. He was sick, and hurting, and grieving, and for a while, he just dropped off the grid. At fifteen years old, I learned just how deep in the hole we were."

Blake's chest ached at the sadness in her voice.

"We were eking out an existence on his disability checks. But he refused to let me sell the house. It was the last place he'd had a home with her. So I did the best I could, supplementing his income by running errands for Trinity, and turning my hand at anything I could find. I discovered I had a knack for refinishing furniture. He would help me sometimes when he was feeling better, and I'd sell the pieces to local antique stores. Sometimes they call and let me know when they have pieces that I can refurbish for them. I've gotten a bit of a reputation for it now."

"That's wonderful, Maddie." Blake had taken so much in his life for granted. He couldn't imagine realizing his family was on the brink of ruin as a teenager and knowing it fell on him to keep them from going over the edge.

"I'm sorry," she whispered.

"Why?" His chest ached at the somber expression in her eyes. They should be happy and smiling, instead of sad all the time.

"I wanted tonight to be special. And it's been nothing but complicated. Everything about us has been complicated."

Blake pushed everything aside in that moment—his own selfishness, shallowness, Abigail, even his own lust for the woman in front of him.

Instead he looked at Madison and really saw her. "No, Maddie. Tonight has really opened my eyes."

She immediately dropped her gaze, but he raised her chin back up with gentle pressure. "I've seen a lot, and I've learned a lot. And it has all told me what an incredibly strong and driven woman you are. That is something to be proud of. And if some guy can't handle it, you kick his ass to the curb."

She gave a huff of laughter. "Yes, sir."

Maddie was a woman to be celebrated. And Blake planned to do just that.

Burying his hands in her hair, he pulled her closer for his kiss. When he came up for air, he whispered, "Don't be sorry, Maddie. You're way more than I ever expected."

This time, he crowded his body close against hers, pressing her into the doorframe. Slowly he rubbed her, up, then down again, imprinting on her just how much he wanted to be with her. Her lips were supple and welcoming, parting in need to invite him in. He dove deep, intent on tasting every inch of her tonight.

In, out and around, he explored her mouth. Nibbled on her lips. Eased his body close to her and away, mimicking the very dance they rushed toward.

He felt her hands roam up his arms, massaging the muscles as she too explored.

She reached his shoulders and dug her fingers in deep, igniting a surge of power that struck hard at the base of his spine. He groaned, needing action. Needing more. He lifted her and almost wept when her legs encircled his waist. "Maddie," he growled. "Please."

"Upstairs," she murmured around kisses that fed the flames.

He took the steps slower than he planned, partly to keep her safe, partly because he couldn't stop kissing her. Maddie's mouth was addictive. Her response egged him on.

She pressed against him, spreading heat through his body in waves, ramping his urgency sky high. He wanted to take his time, wanted to care for her, but he knew the moment was fast approaching when he wouldn't be able to control himself anymore. First, he had to make it good for her.

Maddie deserved more than he could ever give her.

At the top of the stairs, she pointed to an open door down the shadowy hallway. Blake had the barest impression of pale blue walls before he laid her out across the bed. Her face fell into the darkness, but her body was illuminated by the beam of light coming from a lamp left on in the hallway. The green dress she was wearing teased him, leaving him aching for the womanly soft skin it concealed.

With extra care he unbuckled her wedge sandals,

and kissed each ankle bone, celebrating its delicacy. His body screamed at him to hurry, but he clamped down tight and focused on the woman before him.

Maddie.

Lifting one of her leanly muscled legs, he watched as the skirt fell to her waist. He caught a brief glimpse of glittery black material between her legs that had him opening his mouth and brushing his teeth against her calf. Very soon he would taste more of her. She gasped, her muscles twitching beneath his mouth. He repeated the movement closer to her knee, then her thigh, then her inner thigh. Each time she jerked harder, her fingers fisting the pale blanket beneath her. The sound of her gasps in the air was almost as intoxicating as her singing.

Then he buried his face in the heat between her thighs, listening to her cry out as he dragged in her scent with a deep inhale. His brain lit up, sending urgent directives to his body that he struggled to ignore. But his impatient hands grasped the edge of the flimsy material that covered her, ripping it from her hips. He wasn't moving away from her for a single second, not even to remove her panties.

The flesh now laid bare for him was crowned by soft auburn curls. They smelled of musk and some floral scent he couldn't place at the moment. With extra care he parted her lower lips, which were slick with a moisture that had his mouth watering. He opened his lips and pressed against her. Her knees jerked up as if to close off his access, but her hands clenching in his hair sent a different message. Her gasps grew louder, echoing in his ears. Her body throbbed against his tongue. Blake felt himself slipping into a world that was all about Maddie, that revolved around her reactions and his utter need to pull the ultimate high from her.

Her hips lifted against him. He rode her motions out, licking and sucking, instinct taking over. His body throbbed in sympathy to her cries of need.

When her moans reached a fever pitch, he pressed hard, growling his command that she come. Maddie broke against his mouth, one long scream echoing off the walls. It had to be the most satisfying sound Blake had ever heard.

Seven

Maddie lay for long moments, unaware of anything but the pounding of her heart in her ears and the excited throb that dominated her body in this moment. She clutched at the soft blanket beneath her, needing something solid to ground her.

Her very limited experience before hadn't prepared her for the havoc a very focused, very determined man could wreak upon her body. But as satisfied as she was right now, underneath she could feel the return of the urgency. The need to experience the same thing *with* Blake. To return the favor he'd so graciously given her.

He pulled back a little, causing a protest within. He couldn't leave. Not now. Maybe never.

Opening her eyes, she could see him crouched

between her legs. He made no further move away, just silently watched her in the darkness. Slowly she sat up, connecting with his gaze in the dim light. Then she rolled around until she too crouched on her knees. With shaking fingers, she grasped the hem of her dress, lifting it and tossing it to the side. The stream of light from the doorway illuminated her bare body. Only a simple lace bralette covered her breasts. Blake's groan was one of the most gratifying things she'd ever heard. Reaching out, she unbuttoned his shirt, taking her time, letting her fingers brush against his skin. He gasped as she pulled the shirttails loose from his slacks, then ran her fingernails over his chest and belly.

"Please, Madison," he said, breathing as hard as a racehorse.

He made quick work of his belt and zipper, then eased her back against the pillows. To her surprise, he didn't jump right in. Instead he slipped the bralette over her head. Burying his face between her breasts, he squeezed them and played with the pink tips until the fire burned high between her thighs once more. Only then did he take one nipple between his lips and worry the flesh until she squirmed and raised her hips in a plea for more. She cried, clutching at his back through the fine cotton of his shirt. With a growl, Blake tore it from his body and tossed it aside, then pressed down against her.

Flesh to flesh. Heat to heat.

With an urgency that signaled he'd reached the end of his control, Blake used his thighs to press hers even farther apart. She felt him fumble on the condom. Then the blunt tip of him searched and found her core, easing slightly inside. He braced his arms above her shoulders, breathing so hard his chest rubbed against her with every huff. He played for long moments, easing in and out until she thought she would scream in need. He was trying to make it good for her, she knew. But if he didn't enter her soon, she might explode.

Madison needed this to be about them.

Sliding her hands down beneath the edge of his pants, which were miraculously still on, she grasped his clenching muscles and dug deep. At the same time she lifted her hips to him. The feel of him sliding inside her took her breath away. He let himself go all the way to the hilt, then froze. She could feel her body ripple around him, on the cusp of something incredible, something she wouldn't be able to control.

Blake eased his upper body down, letting their skin touch. Then he tucked his mouth against one of her ears. "Hold on, Maddie," he groaned.

Then he started to thrust.

Madison only thought she'd been breathless before. Now every movement forced the air from her lungs. Her body lit up like fireworks. Blake grunted every time their hips met. They strained against each other for that ultimate high. Snapshot sensations imprinted themselves on Madison's mind: the slickness of his skin beneath her fingers; the sound of his voice in her ear; the exquisite pressure of him filling her full. Then he twisted against her and her world exploded.

In the quiet aftermath, listening to the sound of their breathing, it seemed cliché to say she would never be the same again. But Madison knew it to be true.

After long moments, Blake rolled to the side, pulling her with him. In those moments, she had no defense against him. No way to close herself off from the incredible fullness in her heart. Just as she drifted into sleep, she felt the warm pressure of lips against her temple. Blake's words floated around her. "I'll make sure everything is okay, Madison."

Consciousness came slowly to Blake. Normally, he awoke with a start and was out of bed in seconds. Today, the dim light of dawn peeked through the windows as he blinked once, then twice. It took him a moment to realize that Maddie still lay in his embrace.

A first for him.

Usually, as soon as the sex was over, Blake was putting the boundaries back into place. Even if he had to manhandle them back into the grooves. But last night he'd barely slid off Madison, unwilling to get too far from the unbelievably silky skin and the delicate scent of her. He'd pulled her close enough to get the blanket out from under them, covered them with it, then hugged her against his chest in a way he didn't want to acknowledge.

He could tell himself it didn't mean anything, but that didn't change the truth. He was royally screwed.

She still slept deeply. He smoothed back the jumble of her auburn hair so he could see her face, long lashes resting against freckle-sprinkled cheeks. Her lips seemed redder, swollen from their kisses the night before.

He wondered what other evidence he'd left behind. He sure as hell wouldn't be showing any of that to his father.

The memory of his old man left a bitter taste in his mouth. He could go for a cup of coffee…or three…or more. Maybe just the task of fixing it in an unfamiliar kitchen would help him to obliterate the thought of his father demanding proof of his progress?

He might need something stronger, he was afraid.

On his way downstairs, more things than he wanted to think about grabbed his attention. The cracked mirror behind the lamp on the little table in the upper hallway. The closed doors along the hall. Even though he didn't want to, Blake forced himself to open one. All of the furniture had been pushed into the middle of the room and draped. The back wall, which should correspond to the back of the house, had old water stains running down the flowery wallpaper.

He closed the door with a quiet snick and continued downstairs.

A quick glance into a living area opposite the refurbishing room stopped him in his tracks. A worn sofa, rug and coffee table were pushed to one side of the admittedly large room. The other end was occupied by a hospital bed. Bile rose in the back of his throat as Blake took in the area that had been stripped of linens and personal effects, but still bore all the markings of an end-of-life experience. There was a stripped-down bed, a pole to hang fluids on, and what looked like a heart monitor machine on an otherwise plain end table.

While she'd gone to the trouble of cleaning up, Madison hadn't dealt with the bare bones of her father's last days. The thought of her having to deal with this with no support, no helping hands, devastated him. Granted, he hadn't had a true "loved one" in his life, ever, but how had she continued to push forward, day after day, year after year, knowing that she would lose her father?

How devastating.

He forced himself on to the kitchen. Here the true extent of neglect showed in the daylight. Paint was peeling from the walls and windowsill. There was rust on the faucet and inside the sink. Cracks formed a latticework on tile countertop. Blake wasn't an expert in such matters, but he would guess that the house hadn't been properly maintained for a long time and had once been in impeccable quality.

That tile was Italian. The chandeliers were Toso. The kitchen faucet was originally an Axel. No one let that stuff go unless they had to…or strippers came in to take it.

Which could only mean one thing: Madison's family had never sold the Belarus diamond.

Blake crossed over to the budget-brand coffee maker, contemplating the evidence literally before him. Why? Why in the world would her mother keep that diamond and not sell it when they obviously needed the money so badly? Selling that thing on the open market would have set them for life, even if her father's illness had lasted thirty years. Why would she do this?

And what was he supposed to do about it?

This was the last thing he wanted to deal with after last night. As juvenile as it sounded, he wished he could spend his morning sipping coffee and thinking about how good last night had been. Especially if he wasn't going to be allowed to repeat it this morning. But he couldn't.

He had to think about Abigail, about what she was going through, about the fact that she needed him. How did he do that, rather than obsessing about where he went from here?

He hadn't meant for whatever this was between him and Maddie to go this far. He'd planned to get what he needed with as little collateral damage as possible. It was the least risky way of saving Abigail. Despite that, he would never use Madison's body against her.

He wandered back down the hallway to the living room, staring at the large expanse of empty floor between the pieces of furniture.

But now all he could think about was whether she would believe that was exactly what he had done, when the whole story came out. Because he had no doubt it would. He might hope that his father would keep his mouth shut, but that wasn't likely to happen. Especially not if he couldn't have his way.

"What are you doing?"

Blake whirled around to find Madison standing at the foot of the stairs. She had on a thin robe, thin enough for him to tell that she hadn't put on her underclothes. Did that mean she was still open to being vulnerable to him? That was a precious gift Blake wasn't sure he would ever get over.

"I was going to make coffee, then I got distracted."

He knew it sounded lame but it was all he could come up with at the moment. The last thing he wanted to do was make her feel uncomfortable by talking about the empty hospital bed in the room behind him.

She looked so small and frail with her arms wrapped around her ribs like that. He wanted to touch her, to hug her, but her posture was like one big Keep Away sign. She held herself stiffly, her body wound tight. Angled slightly toward him. He noticed she looked everywhere but at the bed.

He wasn't sure how she could even stand to have it in the house, except she probably had no way of moving it. Madison was strong and capable, but not that strong...not strong enough to move that single-handedly...or without a truck.

And he found that he cared, he wanted to help her. Man, he was fully invested.

"Are you ready to go?" she asked.

"Not...really." Blake didn't understood where the

odd question came from. Yes, he'd put on his clothes from last night. He simply wasn't comfortable walking around her house in his birthday suit. He hadn't come prepared for anything else.

She turned and started down the hall, her voice echoing behind her. "I'm sure you're ready to get on the road," she threw over her shoulder. "Clean clothes, a hot shower."

Blake trailed down the hall behind her. What was up with all the questions about leaving? Was she really that eager to see him go?

He stepped through the doorway into the kitchen, where she had turned to face him, her arms crossed tighter than ever across her chest. He struggled not to look down at the effect that had on her breasts, instead focusing on her face.

"Is something wrong?" he asked.

"No." The word was more emphatic than it needed to be.

"You're not going to offer me coffee?" Not that he cared, but he might as well test the waters.

"My father always said my coffee was horrible. You'd probably do better to stop somewhere on your way home."

He was not buying this. He took a step closer to her. Then another. A broken tile shifted beneath his shoe. Madison glanced down, and her lips tightened. So was it the house that was her problem? Or *him* in her house?

Blake took another step. Only this time, Madison stepped back.

He crossed his arms over his chest, mimicking her position. "What's going on, Madison?"

Outwardly he projected calm, seeming in control of this entire situation. But inside, his temperature rose and his heartbeat sped up. He clenched his teeth on a jittery burst of panic. But he wasn't about to walk away. Instead he moved closer.

He should walk away. He knew it. Without a doubt, he should obey the Keep Away sign and leave Madison to herself. He should walk out of this house and never think about her again, and never think about that stupid diamond. But he couldn't.

So he locked away all thoughts of that beautiful jewel and focused on the beauty in front of him. He could divorce himself from his feelings, but then he wouldn't know the pleasure that came with her touch, the comfort that came from her listening ear.

Selfish bastard that he was, he couldn't leave her alone. "Madison, what is it, hon?"

As he came within arm's reach, Blake couldn't resist touching her. He smoothed his thumb across one high cheekbone. Excitement ratcheted up inside him, rapidly overtaking the panic.

Yes, he was definitely a bastard.

She turned her head to look away, only to flinch at whatever she saw. He followed her gaze to see the door to the pantry hanging crooked in its frame. As they stared in silence, the refrigerator struggled, its mechanical hum sounding strained. Blake let his eyelids drift closed for just a moment, wondering if somewhere in his shallow soul he had the words to make her feel better.

He used his hand to turn her head, guide her eyes back around to his. "Madison, it's okay."

She bit her lip, worrying it for minute before releasing the plump flesh. "No, it's not." She glanced up at him through her long, thick lashes. "You're the first person to be in this house since the day my father died."

"You know, if you don't let anyone in, then no one can help you."

"My father always told me we had to help ourselves. We couldn't expect someone else to come in and bail us out."

"But you're only capable of so much, Madison."

"It's amazing what you can be capable of when you're desperate."

He cupped her cheeks between his hands. "You don't have to be desperate anymore."

Her eyes went wide for a moment with a flash of surprise that cut through his shallow soul like a hot knife through butter. If he lived to be hundred, he hoped he never saw that pain in her expression ever again.

But he knew only one way to erase it right now. Holding her still, he bent to capture her lips with his. How could Madison taste so sweet? Last thing at night, or first thing in the morning, she was sweeter than pie. And he was desperate for dessert.

He sampled her lips, their breaths mingling as they gave themselves over to the sensations. He felt

Madison's hands against his back, pulling him closer. To know she wanted him as much as he wanted her sent his spirit soaring. He let his own hands wander down, feeling the heat of her through the thin robe she wore. He groaned against her lips. He needed her. Right now. Not after a walk down the hall to the couch. Not after a walk upstairs to the bed.

Right. Now.

With what little brain he had left, Blake pictured the room in his head. Then he lifted Madison off her feet with his hands around her ribs. Her squeal echoed in his ears. He sat her down on the nearby empty space on the countertop.

He didn't think about where they were. He only thought about her, and the urgency driving him to take her once more.

To his infinite gratitude, she spread her knees wide, making space for him. Blake fumbled in his pocket for a condom, then reached around to lower his zipper. His glance down revealed the shadowed valley between her breasts, visible where her robe had slid open.

Blake drew in a hard, deep breath, easing off the brakes on his drive to be inside her once more. He trailed his fingers along the edges of her robe, sampling the plumpness, feeling her gasp, seeing her nipples tighten beneath the sheer fabric. Slowly he slid one panel to the side, revealing her firm, round breast with its pink-tipped nipple. His mouth watered as he leaned over and licked the turgid tip. Madison arched her back, her breath releasing in a hiss. He licked again. And again. Loving the reaction of her body. Knowing that she'd be wet and ready for him.

He dropped his pants and covered himself for their protection. His fingers found her slick and needy. His heart pounded in his throat as he eased himself through her tightness.

"Oh, Maddie," he moaned. "So good."

Then he felt her legs circle around his waist, trapping him close, pulling him closer. He forced his way in to the hilt, both of them shuddering. He ground against her, his entire body tightening with the need to lose control.

"Please, Blake," she begged.

Holding back was no longer an option. That simple request swept aside his hesitation. He dug deep, gathering every ounce of energy he had, desperate to share something special with her, something he'd never felt with anyone but her. He had a need for her response that would send him over the edge.

He smoothed his hand up her body to her breast, palming, then squeezing it. Tweaking the tip in a way that made her body clamp down on him. She gasped with every thrust but refused to let go.

Blake strained, desperate for release. His hand slid around to her bottom, jerking her against him with every thrust. In his need to impress himself on her, to draw out her response, he buried his mouth against her neck, and sucked on her flesh to make the pounding of her heart match his. She cried out, the sound vibrating against his tongue. Her body squeezed around him, sending his need into hyperspace. He ground against her as they both exploded with an intensity that almost knocked Blake out.

He wanted to crawl inside of her arms and never leave, an idea that at once felt overwhelmingly right and oh-so-wrong in a panicky way. The thought of staying just like this, forever, tempted him.

All too soon, Madison began to shift. He stilled her movements with his hands on her hips. Just a minute more...

"Blake," she murmured. "Your phone."

He blinked. Sure enough, a low metallic ringtone came from his phone, not far away on the countertop. On the display, Blake could see that it was his father's housekeeper. Alarm quickly pushed out the euphoria.

"Blake, it's an emergency." He barely recognized Sherry's shaking voice. "I had to take Abigail to the ER."

Eight

Madison could barely comprehend Blake's mad dash for his clothes. Her brain was still swimming in lust and satiation. Then she got a really good look at his face.

"What's going on?" she asked.

"I've got to go," he murmured. He tried to put a button through the hole on his shirt once, then twice. Finally he swore, then ran his fingers through his hair.

Did she hear him right? "What? Why?"

Who had called? Blake was as unattached as anyone she'd come across, seeming to exist in a strange ecosystem that had no one else living inside of it. Yet after one short conversation he was buttoning his shirt crooked in his haste to leave.

"Blake?"

Still he ignored her, as if his mind were already elsewhere. The switch from having his full attention five minutes ago to being completely tossed aside had her reeling. Not that she expected him to ignore an emergency for her, but what on earth had him switching gears faster than a race car? At least his preoccupation covered her awkward dismount from the counter. She might never look at her kitchen the same way again.

After calling his name a few times, she went to stand between him and the phone he had set back down on the counter while zipping up his pants. "Blake? What is happening?"

"I've got to leave right now." His tone didn't indicate he realized he'd already said this to her before.

"Why?"

He blinked, as if no one had ever asked him that. "They've taken my sister to the hospital."

Sister? "Okay. I'll go with you."

"No."

The vehemence encapsulated in that one word took her aback. "Excuse me?"

"No," he said with a hard shake of his head. "I need to leave now."

The hand he waved at her seemed to indicate it was her lack of clothes that was the problem. But was it? "Blake, you shouldn't go alone. Give me three minutes to throw on—"

"No. Just. Not now."

Hurt shot through Madison with the same speed

that lust had earlier. She was a smart girl. It didn't take her too many tries to realize when someone didn't want her around—whatever the reason. But this wasn't something she could let go. Blake did not look like he should be behind the wheel. Besides, if there was one thing she had experience with, it was hospitals.

She doubted Blake could say the same.

This time she placed her hand over the phone as he reached for it. "Blake."

"What?" he asked, the word sounding short and clipped. He never lifted his eyes from the phone.

"Do you know which hospital?"

That had him glancing up. He gave a short shake of his head.

"When you do, do you know how to get there in the quickest way possible?"

"No," he admitted through clenched teeth.

"Then why don't you find out while I get some clothes on?"

She could actually see the gears start to turn before he gave a quick nod. Madison left him to his phone while she ran upstairs. A quick splash of water on the face was all she dared take the time for, then clean clothes and a ponytail holder she would put her hair in on the way. To her surprise, he was still in the kitchen when she ran in with her tennis shoes in her hand.

"She's at Children's Hospital. Her doctor was already there."

Madison paused for a mere second, then forced herself to finish putting on her shoes. "Let's go."

As much as it hurt, she wasn't surprised when he started to argue on the way to the car. "Just tell me the shortcuts. I'll get myself there."

"And get in a wreck because you're upset behind the wheel."

"I'm perfectly capable of driving right now."

Madison glided around the car until she reached the passenger door, then swung around to face him. "But you are upset, right? Shaken, maybe? In need of a friend?" She grimaced, feeling her anger slip the bounds of her control. "If you don't actually consider me as one, I get it. But I still feel some responsibility to fill that role, since ten minutes ago we were still having sex on my countertop."

Without waiting for an answer, she gave the car hood a quick slap, then slid around the door and into the seat. As she buckled her belt, she called herself every kind of fool. Blake still stood beside the car. Had all of this been just about the sex? If she got any more mixed signals, she wouldn't know which way was up.

Maybe he didn't, either.

Madison tried to hold onto that thought while dragging in a deep breath. For a moment, surprise streaked through her. She'd dealt with any number of medical emergencies in her lifetime…none of which had caused her to lose her cool. Of course, she was usually the person in charge. Not simply along for the ride.

Still, she shouldn't have struck out at him like that.

Thirty seconds later, he slid into the driver's seat. "I'm sorry, Madison—" he started.

"Don't be. Let's just go."

Maybe that wasn't the way to handle this. But she just couldn't go through with helping him if he actually said again out loud that he didn't want her.

She wanted to be a good person who would help him regardless. But she couldn't. Better to just do her part, then deal with the fallout later. After she'd had time to process her own emotions over sleeping with him, then discovering he had a whole family she wasn't aware of. And what man his age had siblings young enough to be treated at Children's Hospital? Was this child really a sister? Or something else?

Madison quickly cut off that line of thinking. She was here. She needed to focus on the job at hand. Speculation would get her nothing but upset.

Madison directed him toward the least busy streets she could think of at this time of the morning. The only saving grace was the absence of school traffic. She watched him closely for any signs that he wasn't in control, but those few moments by himself outside of the car seemed to have calmed him.

She only wished she could get all of her suspicions under control just as easily.

Blake locked down his emotions as tightly as he could, just as tightly as he held the steering wheel. He executed the turns with precision, utilizing every ounce of experience he'd gotten on the autobahn, to maneuver the vehicle without slowing down.

"Call Father's housekeeper," he said, not daring to take his eyes off the road. His phone automatically rang the number, which went straight to voice mail.

Blake wanted to hit something, but he refused to slow down long enough to do so. To his surprise, Madison didn't complain. No gasps, no quick grabs for the door handle. She was just a solid, quiet presence in the car who gave the occasional direction to turn.

"Call Father's housekeeper."

When this call also went to voice mail, he let out a string of expletives that would've had a sailor blushing. Still, Madison remained silent.

"Where is she?" he growled.

Madison pointed out the entryway for the parking deck, and Blake pulled squarely into the valet spot.

Madison waved him through to the ER entrance while she paused next to the valet podium.

Blake felt a flash of gratitude, tossed her the keys, then stepped up his pace to get to the ER desk.

"I need to see my sister. Abigail Boudreaux," he told the nurse at the desk.

A part of him was surprised by the shaky, out-of-breath quality of his voice. This wasn't a Blake that he knew. But he didn't have time to think about that right now. The nurse nodded and calmly asked to see his ID. Her entire demeanor was a counterpoint to his.

Madison arrived as the nurse clicked away on the computer.

"Blake?" she asked. "Isn't there a parent you can call?"

"Good luck getting through to him," Blake murmured. Luckily the nurse looked up before he had to explain his words.

"Sir, I'm afraid I can't help you."

Blake froze. "What do you mean you can't help me? I know my sister was brought here."

Madison tugged at his shirtsleeve, but he ignored her. He focused entirely on the nurse, the person who would get him to his sister the fastest. "I want to see my sister. Abigail Boudreaux."

"I'm afraid I can't help you, sir."

For a moment, Blake was almost certain he was going to climb across the counter. What the hell was going on with him? All he knew was he had to make sure his sister was okay.

Just as Blake opened his mouth to start yelling, Madison intervened. "Blake." Her tone was firm and hard enough to catch his attention. He turned her way.

"Blake," she said in a softer voice. "Let me speak to you for a moment, please."

He gave the nurse a hard stare before following Madison over to the side. "I don't have time for this. I need to see my sister."

"I realize that," Madison said. "The thing is, if you're not listed specifically as someone who should be told she's here, they can't tell you her information. They can't let you up to see her."

"What?"

"It's considered an invasion of privacy and it's against federal regulations. Why don't you try the housekeeper again? Or maybe your father? Your mother?"

He ignored the question implied in her words, and tried to dial Sherry again. The call went straight to voice mail.

Blake felt scattered, like his racing heartbeat was pulling him away from information that was very important but he couldn't focus on. Instead he did the only other thing he knew: he dialed his father again.

"Yes?"

The calm sound of his father's voice only raised his irritation even higher. "Where is Abigail? Are you here at the hospital?"

"Hospital? I don't know what you're talking about."

"The housekeeper called me. Abigail had to be taken to the emergency room but they won't let me see her."

"Well, why would we list you as family? Until recently, I hadn't seen you in nearly twenty years. But I guess that's what the message on my phone is for. I haven't had a chance to listen to it yet."

"She called me almost two hours ago. How come you're not down here?"

"I'm in New York. Besides, it's probably just a fake episode to get attention."

"Abigail's epilepsy is not fake."

Blake knew he was yelling at this point but couldn't control himself. Beside him he sensed Madison shift on her feet. Then a warm weight settled at the small of his back. In all the chaos that raced through his mind and his body, that warm contact became a focal point. Her touch sent a wave of peace over him.

His father was in New York. He wasn't here—not that he would care if he was. Instead of trying to understand that, Blake just hung up the phone. He stared at it in his hand for a moment, wondering if throwing it across the room would make him feel any better. Except it was the only way he could find out any information about Abigail.

"What do I do?" he moaned, bending over to press his palms against his knees. How did he find his baby sister?

"Blake."

The softly spoken word brought his attention back to his surroundings. Blake straightened up, drew in a hard breath, then looked at her. "I need to find her, Madison."

"I know. Let me help you."

Just as she had been since they'd gotten in the car. Her words centered him, just like her touch had. "I don't know what to do."

"What kind of episode did your sister have?"

"She has epilepsy. All the housekeeper said was that she was unresponsive this morning. Maybe some kind of seizure?"

Maddie nodded. Her hand ran down his arm, only

stopping when she reached his hand and curled her fingers around his. "Come with me."

As she headed out the door of the emergency room, he glanced back at the nurse at the desk who watched them walk away. "Wait a minute," he said. "Where are we going?"

Madison paused once they reached the other side of the automatic doors. Then she looked up at him. "I know of another waiting room for pediatrics that might be helpful. Let's go in the front of the hospital and see if we can possibly find the housekeeper there. That'll be the quickest way," she said, "even though it doesn't seem like it. Badgering the nurse will get us nowhere. I know—I have plenty of experience."

He walked with her along the sidewalks outside the huge buildings. Impatience bubbled up inside of him, but there were no other options for him at this moment. "How do you know this?" he asked.

"The staff at Maison de Jardin sometimes has to come to the hospital to help residents who've been injured, whose spouses have abused them. And their children." She tossed him a quick glance. "I've been here quite a few times."

She maintained a quick pace, not letting her shorter stature keep her from matching his longer strides. "Plus some of our residents actually come to work here."

Blake paused a step. "Can't you ask one of them to help us?"

"Unfortunately no. I can't ask them to risk their

jobs when they've worked so hard to get into a better place."

As much as the logic made sense, Blake could only see as far as his needs in this moment.

Madison led him in the front door proper and took him around to a large bank of elevators. No sooner were they in one than she hit the button for the third floor.

"Has your...sister...always had epilepsy?"

There it was, the guilt that he couldn't figure out how to shake. "I don't know. I know this particular diagnosis is recent, but I'm not sure how long her symptoms have been occurring."

He shifted on his feet, uncomfortable with the knowledge that he had no idea what was happening, he had no control over the situation, and if he ever found that blasted diamond, he would find himself completely responsible for a child with an illness that could land her in the hospital. What the hell was he even doing here?

They came out of the elevator to a long hallway. Madison rushed down until it opened into a nurses station. "Tamika," she exclaimed. "I wasn't sure if you were working today."

Blake paused behind her as the young black woman in scrubs gave him a good eyeing.

He simply stared back.

"What are you doing here, Madison?" she asked.

"We're looking for... Blake's sister. I was just going to take him across to the waiting room."

Hearing her words, Blake turned abruptly and

saw a waiting room behind them. He strode across the hall into the doorway.

"Mr. Boudreaux!"

Blake was so relieved to see Sherry rising from one of the chairs that he thought he might melt into a puddle. "Where is she?" he asked, rushing over to help her. "Is she okay?"

"Oh, Mr. Boudreaux. They haven't come to tell me anything." Tears overflowed the woman's eyes to trickle down her cheeks. "I can't imagine that little poppet all alone."

So he was one step closer but still knew nothing. Soon Blake found himself with an armful of weeping housekeeper, and his fear for his sister was even higher than ever.

Nine

"Is that really him?" Tamika asked, straining her neck to see behind Madison into the waiting room.

"Stop it." Madison wasn't sure how she felt about Blake in this moment, but she certainly didn't feel comfortable with her friend ogling him. She drew in a calming breath, only to wince at the antiseptic scent of the hospital halls. "We're just trying to find out where the little girl is. The housekeeper brought her in. All I know is that it has something to do with her epilepsy."

"Why would a housekeeper bring her in? Where are the parents?" Tamika asked, bracing her hands on her hips. Tamika's passion lay in caring for the children on this floor—and making sure none of them were mistreated.

Madison shook her head. "Blake tried to call someone while we were downstairs. I guess his father? I'm really not sure. It sounded like he might be out of town."

"How could he not have any information about his child? Are you sure this little girl is his sister?"

Madison did not want to go there. "I've been told very little."

Tamika looked sideways at her for a moment, confirming Madison's own fears.

"That's all I know. He tried to call the housekeeper and couldn't get her on the phone."

"Cell reception up here is terrible," Tamika said. "Her phone probably wouldn't work in that waiting room."

"That's what it sounds like." Madison glanced over her shoulder to see Blake holding a woman wearing a maid's uniform in his arms. "But I'm guessing he's found her now."

Her friend grumbled beneath her breath as she watched them. Then Madison and Tamika shared a glance. Madison felt awkward. She'd done what she told Blake she would. Should she join him now? The housekeeper appeared to be crying, definitely distraught. Should she offer some kind of help?

"I don't know what to do," Madison said. *About any of it*, but she didn't say that part out loud. She guessed maybe she could have gone online and looked into his family, but the excruciating effect of the gossip surrounding her friend Trinity had left a bad taste in her mouth. Besides, she hadn't wanted anything else to mess with her self-esteem. Guess she'd shot herself in the foot there?

"Should I go in there? Should I ask if I can help?"

"Girl, I'd help him all day long," Tamika teased with a saucy wink. "He's very pretty. Even prettier in person than he was online."

"Tamika!"

"Well, he is." She offered her typical shrug when she was misbehaving, then glanced over her monitors for a moment.

"Don't you have a job to do?"

"Not at the moment. All's quiet."

"We need to find you a boyfriend," Madison grumbled. Then maybe she would stay out of Madison's love life.

"Well, if Blake has any friends…"

She'd walked right into that one. She gave her friend a quelling look. "I'm serious, Tamika. I had no idea he even had a sister. He hasn't spoken much about his family."

"What do you talk about?"

At first Madison thought she was being facetious again, but then realized her friend was serious. "We've talked about my family, the house, my job."

"But he's giving no information about himself?" She shook her head. "Girl, you'd better be careful."

Madison knew that. She just didn't know if she was in a position to be careful anymore. Blake's possession of her body had sealed what her spirit already knew. But was he on the same page?

He'd said he wanted to be with her. But he hadn't

really shared himself with her, had he? Other than his art, and hints that his childhood had been quite bad, he hadn't really shared much. It was all about the present…and her. Looking back, that didn't seem right.

"I recognize that expression," Tamika said. "I see more cookies in our future."

Madison arched an eyebrow at her friend but was afraid Tamika wasn't far from right. "Any requests?"

"You know I'm good with any chocolate, and I've got finals coming up."

"I'm glad my pain can feed your success." Madison could already feel the depression sinking in. She should have known that last night was too good to be true.

"I hope not," Tamika said, a frown between her brows. "I know I tease you a lot, but you're the last person who deserves any more grief."

Madison wished she could hug her friend, but the nurses station desk between them prevented that. "Thank you, Tamika."

"My pleasure."

Then a patient pressed a call button in one of the rooms and Tamika went to answer it. Madison stared after her friend for long moments. She'd been so blessed in her life. Yes, she'd lost both her parents. But they'd been a blessing to her while they'd been alive. And her friends, they helped keep her going. She drew in a deep, long breath. She could only do what she knew, which was to help people, including Blake. That was what she would do for now. The rest could be worried about later. She turned back toward the waiting room, only to find it empty.

She glanced up and down the hallway, but it too was empty. The faces at the nurses station were now unfamiliar, as Tamika had left to answer the call.

Madison stood in confusion for long moments. Where had Blake gone? Why didn't he let her know?

Of course, he hadn't wanted her here in the first place. Maybe taking her with him was more information than he wanted to let her in on. This was definitely a new one, and only magnified her impression from earlier that he'd been holding parts of himself back. Possibly hiding his true self on purpose.

What reason could he have for doing that? No good ones that she could think of.

She'd never heard of being dumped at the hospital. Then again, she'd served her purpose, hadn't she? She glanced at her phone. Sure enough, no reception.

So calling him was out. She could stand around and wait for him to get back, but did he want her here? Somehow the thought of sitting here for hours on end while Tamika was working and knew she'd been dumped was just more than she could handle. She'd be more productive at home, where she knew her place and had things to do.

So she headed downstairs. As she stood in the lobby, she called for a cab.

The debate raged within her as she waited. Should she tell him? Should she not tell him? Should she let him make the next move? In the end, she couldn't not say something. Just disappearing without a word wasn't a responsible action on her part. So she typed out a text letting him know she'd gone home.

By the time she'd pulled into the driveway, the screen of her phone was still empty. Just as empty as she was.

Madison put a little extra effort behind her sandpapering. Normally she would have used an electric sander, but she'd chosen to do the manual work on the details simply to keep herself from thinking. It had been twenty-four hours since she'd walked out of the hospital, and Blake had still not contacted her.

She'd gone to work and kept herself busy with files, calls and orders. No one had been hanging around, so she didn't see the point in baking. She'd be tempted to just eat all the cookie dough herself. So by midafternoon, she'd come home and tried to keep herself busy on a new antique dresser that she'd gotten from one of the specialty stores in town. Unfortunately, it wasn't wearing her out as much as she'd like.

But she was too wound up to settle into reading her mother's journals, and nothing on TV interested her. So she'd rather get her hands roughed up and be productive at the same time, instead of spending her time pining over someone who couldn't care less about her.

She did recognize the selfishness in her thoughts. Blake was really concerned about his sister, and she hoped that the little girl was okay. She hoped that his not contacting her didn't mean that something terrible had happened to the child. But how long did it take to send a simple text?

Caring about someone meant you let them know you were okay. She could take the hint.

So she scratched and scraped, going with the grain to preserve the wood underneath the tacky finish and layer of old paint. She knew in the end she would create something that was really beautiful, and that kept her going.

She just wished she could shut off her brain for a few minutes.

Just then her phone dinged. Madison glanced over at it for a moment, not sure if she really wanted to see what was on it. All this time she'd been mentally complaining that he hadn't contacted her, and now she wasn't even sure she wanted to see if it was him, or what he had to say.

Finally, she dropped the piece of sandpaper, and wiped the dust from her arms. Then she took the few steps to pick up her phone and read the screen.

I'm at the gate.

Well, at least Blake was being considerate. The lock on the gate was so old he probably could've pushed it open without even worrying about letting her know. Instead he'd at least given her a heads-up.

Madison wasn't sure what she wanted. This whole relationship had been like a roller coaster. Did she want to let him in? She knew she cared, or else she wouldn't have spent the last twenty-four hours obsessing over him not contacting her. But was this a matter of too little too late?

Curiosity finally got the better of her, and she stepped outside to unlock the gate. They'd never been able to afford a fancy electronic version, so she had to manually pop the lock to let him in.

By the time he drove through, parked the car and got out, she'd closed the gate behind him and was standing at the entrance to the kitchen. The heat outside caused sweat to bead along her hairline. But she wasn't about to let him in this house without a really good reason.

"Hey, Maddie. How's it going?"

For a moment she simply stared at him. Did he really think he could leave her hanging for twenty-four hours and just waltz back in with a hearty how-you-doin'?

"You don't get to call me Maddie anymore."

That wasn't what she'd expected to come out of her mouth, and apparently he hadn't, either. The surprise on his face was clear, and for a moment she felt ashamed. What she'd said hadn't been polite, but then she realized at least it was true. Maddie was a nickname that came with intimacy. Intimacy meant relationship. Relationship meant including someone in your life.

"I'm sorry," he said, and it actually seemed true. "I didn't mean to upset you."

"Then why would you completely blank me out for twenty-four hours? Why wouldn't you at least send a text letting me know if you were okay, if your sister was okay?"

For a moment, his entire expression shut down. His body stiffened as if he would pull away from her. *This is it. We're done.*

Then he took a deep breath and said, "Maddie, um Madison." He shook his head. "You're right. I'm going to go out on a limb and be honest here and say it didn't occur to me that you would want me to hear from me with an update."

"Why?"

Blake wiped the sweat off his forehead. "I know this doesn't reflect well on me but frankly, I've never been in a relationship before. I've never been involved with a woman who would want to know those things. And even if she did, I wouldn't have a clue how to give them to her." He took a step back. "And I also haven't been involved with my family in many years. Dealing with a crisis like this is out of my realm of experience, and it never occurred to me that you would want to be involved, either."

Well, at least he'd been honest. As the seconds ticked by, Maddie just stood there, numb as she tried to understand what living like that could possibly be like. How could you go through life with no one around who cared anything about you? How could you not have contact with your family? Blake seemed to care a lot about his little sister. How had that happened?

One thing at a time. "Blake, it wouldn't matter if we weren't involved. I would still want to help you.

I would still care about what happened to your sister. I would still want to help support you. I thought I'd made that clear."

"That's because you're a much better person than me."

"I'm not an angel. I'm just human."

"Then we'll agree to disagree."

"So I don't know what to do here. What is it that you want me to do? Back off?"

Because that really was not in her wheelhouse. Thankfully, he was already shaking his head.

"Do you want me to not ask questions?"

"I'm guessing that might be impossible for you." His grin had a touch of smirk.

Time to bring her fears to the fore. "Well, I don't really think it's fair that you get to pry into my life and I don't get to pry into yours."

The widening of his eyes told her she'd hit a nerve. Then he gave a short nod. "I'm gonna try, Madison."

"Would you rather walk away now?" Because he obviously wasn't comfortable with this.

As if something inside him was unleashed, Blake sprung forward to wrap her in his arms. He buried his face into her neck. "No. No. No," he murmured against her skin.

Madison's resistance melted away. Blake was different than anyone she'd known, and she just had to work with that. Not accept it. But figure out what that meant for both of them.

She pulled him into the semi-cool house, which was a bit of a relief after the heat of the Louisiana sun outside. He closed the door behind him, then sank to his knees in front of her. He buried his face against her belly. Madison wrapped her arms around his shoulders, the weight of her heart telling her she was seeing him in this moment like no one else ever had.

"I thought I was going to lose her," he said. He didn't look up. He didn't say anything more. And she knew he was admitting something he might not have to anyone else.

"Is she going to be okay?"

He nodded against her. "I never thought I'd get this attached to a child. But she's so small, so fragile. Seeing her in that hospital bed…"

She felt the tremor that shook him and rubbed his back. "How long has she been sick?"

"From what I understand, she was diagnosed several months ago with the epilepsy. Her mother never said anything about it before."

So she had a mother and father, but the housekeeper took her to the hospital? "Where were her parents?"

"My father was in New York. He and my mother divorced long ago. Abigail's mother is who knows where in Europe. How she could leave a seven-year-old like that is beyond even me."

Madison clutched him a little closer, disbelief sweeping over her. How in the world could they do that? Blake's horror made a little more sense now. Wait—

"Blake, is this the family business that brought you home?"

He nodded but didn't say more. Madison imagined this little conversation was the most Blake had shared with anyone, ever. While she should probably be nervous about that, she couldn't help but be grateful that she was someone he felt comfortable sharing this burden with.

After a few long moments, Blake stood and pressed a soft kiss against her lips. "Madison?" he murmured.

She knew what he was asking, without him having to say the words. And she knew what she wanted, without needing any promises.

So she once more took his hand in hers and led him up the stairs to her room. There she pulled her dusty T-shirt over her head and unsnapped her bra so it could fall away. She peeled off her khaki work pants and the plain pair of panties underneath. The whole time Blake watched her, his gaze ravenously devouring every new inch of bare skin she revealed. His fingers played over her, as if using his fingertips to memorize every curve and valley. Her breath caught as he lingered at the tips of her breasts, at the curve of her hips, at the apex of her thighs.

He tore his own clothes off with more haste than decorum, slid on protection and covered her body with his. As he slipped inside her, Madison squeezed her eyes shut, hoping to hide the sheen of tears caused by the emotions welling inside her. Somehow she knew she'd made a choice tonight. There were no guarantees for how it would turn out. But with every thrust he made her his. There was no turning back, only going forward. She didn't know how to do that. But she guessed she'd take it one day at a time.

As he took them both over the edge, she squeezed her arms around him, hugging him close, and silently accepted that despite all the craziness, this was the man for her.

Still she couldn't stop herself from asking, as they lay entwined on her bed, "Blake, is there anything else I need to know?"

Why didn't the shake of his head make her feel any better?

Ten

Blake was surprised when Abigail let him lift her from the car and into his arms. Sherry stood nearby as he carried her to the door. It was amazing how light she felt against him, how fragile. The doctor had said that she wasn't in any more danger, but that didn't take away the fear.

Blake knew the minute they stepped through the front door that his father was home. Yes, it could've just been the cold feel of the house after decades of being possessed by his father, but somehow he knew the concentration of his father's essence when he was around. It was an awareness he'd never get rid of.

Blake ignored the movement in his peripheral vision as he crossed the foyer, and continued toward the stairs. Abigail deserved to be at home, in her own bed, happy and safe. At least he could provide that.

He settled her into her bed and covered her with a comforter. The trusting expression in her brown eyes reached into his chest and squeezed. "It's going to be okay, Abigail." He hoped he sounded more confident than he was. Either way, Abigail got the short end of the stick.

"Thank you, Blake."

"Sleep well, sweetheart." Blake tucked the blanket in around her again, not sure if that was actually how this was done. Then he left the housekeeper to supervise bedtime.

He came back down the stairs with a feeling of dread. But this time it wasn't just about seeing his father. It was the knowledge that he couldn't keep either of the girls in his life safe from Armand. And he had no idea what to do about that.

"Blake, I see you found your way home again."

For a split second, Blake considered walking straight out the door. Not pausing. Not acknowledging his father in any way. But the memory of that little girl in his arms stayed his steps.

"Well, for now I don't have any choice, do I?"

His father inclined his head as he stepped farther into the foyer. "So how much did this hospital visit cost me?"

Even for his father, that seemed like a crass question. So Blake didn't bother to suppress his sarcasm. "Don't worry, Dad. I took care of it for you."

"I'm amazed they let you, considering they didn't want to give you access to her at all."

That gave Blake a little jolt but he said, "They'll take money under any circumstances."

His father nodded; obviously Blake had finally learned to speak his language. He took a few steps toward the front door.

"At least it wasn't an inconvenience to you," Blake said, looking back over his shoulder at his father.

"That's right."

That smirk made Blake want to wipe it off his face. But his father was ready to move on to new sport.

"So you finally bagged her, did you?"

Blake stopped dead in his tracks, struggling to keep his face completely blank as rage swept over him. To hear Madison spoken about in the same way teenagers would talk about a girl in a locker room was infuriating. What they had shared had nothing to do with bagging and everything to do with discovering who they each were. Blake couldn't even believe he thought about it in those terms, but it was true.

Then he realized the implications of what his father had just said, and swung around to face him head on. "What do you mean? What have you heard?"

Blake knew that his father had no friends who were close to Madison or her family or the charity. So who would be gossiping about them with him? Especially since his father had been in New York. "What did you do, Father?"

"The same thing any father does when his son cuts him out of his life. I hired a private detective."

"What the hell? Who spies on their child? What happened to 'show me proof'? Like my last visit."

Armand shook his head. "Your proof is not very reliable. And I know the closer you get to the girl, it will be even less so. Or the closer you get to Abigail. So I went with an unbiased source."

"Hell, if you're going to go to those lengths, why don't you just have someone break into her house and steal the diamond?"

Blake quickly bit his tongue, even though it had to have been an idea that his father thought of long ago. But the thought of Maddie being subjected to someone breaking into her house freaked him out.

"Stealing is illegal," his father said matter-of-factly, as if every machination he'd imposed since Blake had returned home wasn't in some way evil. But it was legal, and thus acceptable. Then Armand went on, "If the diamond is obtained through illegal means that can be tracked back to me, it will be difficult to sell."

"So you want me to steal it instead?"

"Actually, I figure she'll just hand it over to you. Or, if you take something she never knew she had, then is it really stealing?"

Blake shoved the completely insane reasoning behind his father's words away, and focused on the most pressing issue. "I can't believe you had someone spying on me."

And that person had been spying on Madison,

too. The sheer weight of that understanding hit him hard. The things he was bringing into Maddie's life weren't just unfair to her. This was an invasion of massive proportions. He just hoped he could live with the results.

"You will stay away from Maddie," he insisted. "Do you understand me?"

His father only answered with another smirk. In that moment, a large part of the old Blake reappeared. The urgent need to run, to escape, just as he had when he was seventeen, was overwhelming. The only thing that kept his feet planted right where he was was a little girl upstairs and a woman across town, neither of whom he could abandon. When he'd walked out of here as a teenager, he couldn't give a rat's ass about anybody else. There was no one to care about. Every person in his life had disappeared, just like they had out of Abigail's life. But now he refused to run out on her like others had.

But he just wasn't sure how to help her.

"Don't worry, you bastard. You'll get what you want."

But as he walked out, Blake knew he was biding time. He had to find a way out of the situation and quick. And that way out couldn't involve stealing a diamond, even one Madison didn't know she had.

I had options. When I chose to be with my husband, I knew what I was giving up. But not the pain that would follow.

I knew the man I was leaving behind would be

*vindictive, and I knew I would be punished, but I had
no idea he would take it out on my family like this.*

Madison read the lines once more. Many times
her mother had mentioned making choices, but for
the most part her words were about routine decisions.
This was the first Madison had read about a vindictive *man*. What did that mean?

A quick glance over at the clock told her that
Blake would be here any moment. He had offered
to take her to an event at the ASTRA Museum that
Trinity hadn't been able to attend. Madison wanted
to make a good impression. To represent the charity in the best way possible. Hopefully, with Blake
by her side, things would go smoothly. They'd be no
embarrassment or fumbling.

She needed to get her shoes on before he arrived.
She set the journal on her bedside table and crossed
to her closet. Just as she reached it, she heard the
book tumble to the floor. Crossing back, she picked
it up to return it to the table, only to have something
fall from the back.

It looked like several pieces of paper folded together. Madison could see her mother's handwriting
on the back of the outside sheet. That was odd. She'd
never found anything more than bookmarks stuck
into her mother's journals. Only she didn't have time
to look at it right now. She laid the packet on top of
the journal and returned to the closet for her shoes.

When she went outside a few minutes later,
Blake's wolf whistle made her smile as she crossed
over to the car. She slid into her seat and was sur-

prised when he leaned across for a quick kiss. This felt more like a real date. So far she and Blake seemed to only have out-of-the-ordinary times together. But this felt real and good. Madison would be more than happy to have a quiet, normal date.

"So," he said as he got them on the road, "I was wondering how you would feel about meeting my little sister."

For a moment, Madison felt like a bomb had exploded in the car. She glanced over at him as if to say, *Did you feel that?* The only indication that his request was unusual even for him was his super tight grip on the steering wheel.

So he knew what he was doing, and the fact that he was willing to still do it filled her with excitement. She also felt a touch of nervousness, because what did she know about spending time with a seven-year-old? Granted, she'd spent plenty of time with children at Maison de Jardin. But she had a feeling that, like Blake, his little sister would be a whole different breed of people.

"What did you have in mind?"

Blake chuckled. "I was hoping you could tell me. I've rarely spent time with her except overseas and then we weren't really doing kid stuff. She seemed fascinated by me probably because everything else about being in Europe bored her."

Madison laughed. "I doubt that. I find you fascinating all the time."

Her heart sped up when he reached over and

squeezed her hand. It felt so normal, so right. Madison wondered if she had a right to be this happy.

"What does your sister like to do?"

"I have no idea. I think she likes animals? She seems pretty girlie. Likes dresses and the color pink."

"Maybe we could take her to City Park? It's not too hot if we go in the morning. They have some animals, playgrounds and lots of shade there." Was that too mundane for this child? It was going to be a long day if Madison worried herself over everything. She just had to stop and treat Abigail like any other kid she was taking on an adventure.

"Sure. Then maybe lunch out?"

"Good." Madison tried not to sound out of breath. This would be good.

She was really starting to relax and enjoy their time together after checking in at the museum and talking with a few people she already knew. Blake's ability to carry a conversation in a social setting really helped her relax. She knew she shouldn't be dependent on having a wing man, but it wouldn't hurt for these first few events, right?

She reminded herself of that as he excused himself to go make a call to check on Abigail. Sherry had been scared enough by the events the other day that she now gave him regular updates, despite whatever her boss might say. Madison's mind was just boggled by the thought. Blake hadn't come right out and said it, but Madison could tell that his father had to be emotionally abusive or highly manipulative. She had too much experience with these types of situations to not have a strong suspicion about what was going on.

She strolled around the rotunda in the museum, studying the various paintings highlighted here. It was a gorgeous space, one that she enjoyed standing in for a while whenever she visited the ASTRA. As she stood in front of one particular painting, a voice interrupted her thoughts.

"I never realized how much you look like your mother."

Startled, Madison whirled around to find herself facing a man of average height, looking slick in a black suit and blue tie that matched his vividly hued eyes. She was startled, because his eyes were exactly like Blake's, except cold where Blake's were heated.

The man studied her a moment more, then said, "Remarkable." He held out his hand. "My name is Armand."

"Madison, Madison Landry." She sounded out of breath to her own ears, and quickly tried to regain her poise.

"I am aware. Your mother was a beautiful woman, in a class by herself."

Madison shifted on her heels. Though the man was smiling, she felt uneasy. "How did you know her?"

All that Madison knew about her mother's life, outside of her own interactions with her, was from her journals. Which didn't touch on anything before her marriage, except her relationship with her elderly parents. Curiosity swept through her despite her nerves. After all, no one that she'd met at these events had mentioned knowing her mother, despite their pretty strong resemblance.

"Your mother was well known in my social circles," he said, his slight Cajun accent making the words sound exotic. "Before she…removed herself."

Again the man's intense gaze gave her a slight sense of déjà vu. Where was Blake? Suddenly she wanted him with her right now.

"Her beauty would have lit up any social setting, her grace a complement to any household."

Why did it sound like he was talking about Jacqueline as if she were an object? "My mother was a very gracious, caring woman."

With one elegant brow arched, his expression turned almost cold. "That I wouldn't know."

"Then you must not have met her in person." So many people's lives had been touched by her mother's authentic nature. But she also knew that those types of interactions didn't really make themselves known in this kind of social setting.

As if he read her mind, he said, "Circumstances often dictate what we learn about a person."

True, but that was kind of a strange thing for him to say to her. Madison found herself unconsciously taking a step back and forced herself to be still.

She'd been curious about her mother's life before her marriage for so long that she wanted to ask questions. She'd never met someone who knew her mother then. But something about the man's demeanor, the cold way he spoke, kept those questions locked inside.

Out of the corner of her eye, she saw Blake pass through the doorway into the arch. Relief swept over her.

Blake's eyes widened as he approached. She hadn't been mistaken. His blue eyes matched the colder ones of the man in front of her, who was staring her down as if she were a subject to be studied rather than a person to be known.

"Father!"

The steel behind Blake's voice startled her.

Armand turned slowly to face his son. Madison was surprised to see Blake's expression go from anger to almost a total blank. As if he completely locked himself down in his father's presence.

"Son, how could you leave such a beautiful woman unattended and vulnerable?"

There it was. That sense that though the words were innocuous, the meaning behind them was almost a threat. Why was that?

As Blake approached, he stepped right up to Madison's side, closer than he had all afternoon, and placed his hand squarely at the small of her back. The connection helped steady her skyrocketing emotions.

Given her knowledge of Blake's family, she had no doubts that Armand was an abuser. Whether he'd physically attacked the children, she wasn't sure. But the rise of the hair at the nape of her neck meant she sensed danger in his presence. Instinctively she braced her legs and straightened her back, as if she expected him to fly at her at any moment.

"I was checking with Sherry on Abigail. Remember her?"

It was hard to imagine this man as the father of a seven-year-old. It explained a lot about Blake. And made her heart ache for Abigail.

"Oh, yes. She's been most…helpful."

Madison felt like she was listening to a conversation where half the dialogue was missing. As if father and son were communicating telepathically. She could feel her hackles rise despite the innocuous words. What was happening here? It almost seemed as if they were silently challenging each other in a quest for dominance she didn't understand.

Alarms were going off in her head despite how calm everyone was. She knew without a doubt this man should not be left alone with the child.

She wasn't sure why, but that was why she had instincts. Something they taught the tenants at Maison de Jardin to never discount. Her heart raced. She wanted to be anywhere but under this man's gaze.

Blake didn't even look in her direction. He kept his eyes trained on his father, as if one look away might allow him to strike. Somehow Blake's watchfulness kept his father in check.

"She is indeed beautiful," his father said.

Suddenly Madison realized he was talking about her, but as if she weren't really here.

"I can understand your fascination with her. Just

remember your duty. And that bloodlines tell a much bigger story," the older man continued.

Then Armand turned abruptly away and walked back down the gallery to disappear out the doorway. Madison shivered. As her instincts continued to ping and prod, she knew one thing for certain: she hoped she never ran into that man again.

"Family is something, huh?" Blake said.

"A little strange." That was the nicest way Madison knew how to put it. But she couldn't just go around insulting his father.

"Oh, he's an odd bird all right."

But she couldn't shake the feeling that Blake had been trying to protect her somehow. Especially when he'd put his hand against the small of her back. It could've just been a polite gesture, but the firm pressure of the contact seemed to have a different meaning. He wasn't trying to direct her somewhere. Instead, it was almost as if he were trying to reassure himself that she were okay.

It echoed her own uneasy intuition around his father. A high adrenaline rush, as if she'd had a face-to-face with one of the abusers Maison's tenants sought shelter from.

"Abigail isn't safe with him," she said, murmuring almost as if to herself.

Blake jerked to a halt, turning to her and stepping close. "What did you say?"

She looked up into his eyes and wondered if he would accept the truth. A lot of people who had abusers in their lives didn't. But she didn't do what she did every day to make friends. "Blake, I know he's your father, but there's something not right about him."

"You're not telling me anything I didn't already know."

Relief slipped through her. "So you know Abigail isn't safe there. Especially without her mother."

She felt his hand go tense on her back, the fingers digging in on either side of her spine. Not in a painful way, but almost as if he were having a reaction he couldn't control. "I'm working on that."

As she stared up at him, and realized he was a thirtysomething playboy with no experience of children trying to do what he could to help his seven-year-old half sister, pride swelled within her. He didn't have to help. He wasn't Abigail's primary caregiver. She had parents. He could've just walked away and ignored it.

"I'm proud of you," she said.

The breath seemed to almost whoosh from his body. He swallowed hard, and his eyes darkened with emotion. The frown that appeared was sad in and of itself. How few people had said thank-you to him that it would upset him?

"I'm just trying to do my best," he said.

Just then they were interrupted by the waiter asking if they wanted a drink.

Madison kept her gaze on Blake, letting a small smile play at her lips. Her protector. She couldn't be in better hands, could she?

Eleven

Blake eased back into Madison's bed, pulling her close up against his chest when she shifted in her sleep. Dawn was just lightening the sky behind the window shades, but he'd been up for hours.

He'd done his best to do a thorough search of the house. Every step felt like a betrayal, after Madison had asked him to stay the night following their trip to the museum.

He felt like his entire conversation with Madison after his father left had been a big huge lie. He was worried about Abigail; he was trying to find a way to help her, but he couldn't come right out and tell Madison that after his father had been sending him a warning earlier.

Don't get too close to Madison. Because I will

take her out one way or another. All over what her mother did to me. Or maybe his father was just being like this to prove that Blake could not control him in any way. Madison would never be safe. So he'd done the very thing he didn't want to do, and searched her house during the night.

Of course, he hadn't found anything. No secret cubbies, no safes. Nothing that would indicate a multimillion-dollar diamond was hiding somewhere on the premises. He'd searched every room, looked into every crevice. All the while his heart pounding, afraid Madison would walk in and he'd have to explain himself.

He was already sick at the thought that someday soon she'd know why he was here. Or rather she would assume she knew the real reason, though it had changed for him. Because if the last couple of hours had taught him something, it was that he didn't want to hurt Madison. He loved her. And that knowledge had sent him straight back to her arms. He didn't know what else to do, just like he didn't know what else to do with Abigail.

He'd searched his mind for ways out of the situation. Hell, he'd even made a phone call in the middle of the night to Abigail's mother. To no avail, because the woman wasn't answering…just like she hadn't any time in the last week as he'd tried to contact her. She probably figured he would deride her for walking out on her child. But he just needed a solution.

One that didn't involve the Belarus diamond. Because time was running out. And Blake had no more leads.

So instead he buried his head in the sand. Or rather, in Madison's fragrant hair. He breathed her in, and even though his body stirred, he was content to lie there with her in his arms. Right now he had no way to delay the inevitable, but by God he'd find a way to leave her with something good.

By the time the sun had fully risen, and Madison began to stir in his arms, he knew exactly what he wanted to do with his day. He gave her a chance to wake up, and felt his whole body react when she blinked at him with sleepy eyes.

"Good morning," she murmured.

"Yes. Yes it is," he replied. And he planned to make the most of it. "Want me to make you some coffee?"

She nodded, and he slid from the bed. The glance over his shoulder as he walked to the door revealed a warm, sleepy woman stretching beneath a light sheet. He almost turned back, so that he could explore the soft curves and erect nipples beneath the thin covering. But he knew then he might never get back out. So Blake headed down the stairs with a chuckle.

He waited until she had a whole cup of the chicory brew in her before he broached the subject. "So what are the plans for today?" he asked.

"Oh, I don't have to be over at the charity today. I figured I'd putter around with the furniture."

"I have something a little different in mind."

She lifted a brow as she stared at him over the

rim of her newly refreshed cup. She took a sip before asking, "And what would that be?"

"What exactly do you want to do with that hospital bed?"

He knew the question was unexpected but didn't realize how much until she set her mug down on the counter with a hard *thunk*. Coffee sloshed over the side and unto the marble tile countertop. Her voice was huskier than usual when she asked, "Why do you ask?"

Blake knew he had to tread very carefully here. "I'm just wondering. Has it not been moved because you need it for some reason? Or because you need help with it?"

She turned her gaze over his shoulder to stare out the kitchen window. The way her lips tightened for a moment he thought she wouldn't answer, but then she said, "I certainly have no need for it anymore. I know what I want to do with it, but I just…"

Her voice trailed off in a way that made him sad for her. He knew she didn't want to admit that she wasn't capable of something, but they both knew the truth.

It was right there in her sad smile when she returned her gaze to meet his. "So I just cleaned it up as best I could, and I'll get around to it when I get around to it," she said with a shrug.

"Well, how about we get around to it today? What is it you want to do?"

She quickly let her lashes fall, covering the expression in her eyes. "I don't understand. Why would you want to do this today? Or at all? We could do anything. Take your sister to the park today. I could bake. Any number of things that wouldn't be—"

"Hard?"

She glanced back up at him, her teeth worrying her lower lip.

"I know it's hard, Madison. And I just want to help." He held up hands that had no callouses or signs of manual labor. "I can't paint. I could get up on the roof, but I wouldn't know what to do when I got there."

He was encouraged by her small smile.

"But this, I can help with. I just want to lighten the load a little bit."

To his surprise, she covered her face with her hands. Panic whittled its way through him as her shoulders shook. *No. Not crying.* That was the last thing he knew how to handle.

He stood awkwardly for a couple of seconds, unsure what to do as her sobs got louder. Was he totally out of line?

In the end, he just couldn't bear to see her standing there, sobbing and holding herself upright on her own. It seemed to be the epitome of Madison's life. That she handle every emotion, every circumstance *alone*. So he stepped forward and put his arms around her shoulders. He didn't know if it was the right move, he only knew he had to do it.

She leaned into him, her body seeking him out. Her hands dropped from her face and encircled his back. She buried her face against his chest, and the noise slowly subsided. With no other direction, Blake simply rested his hand on the back of her neck and held her. All too soon she pulled away, keeping her face averted as she walked over to grab a paper towel and blow her nose.

"Well, that was attractive," she said.

Blake appreciated her desire to brush off the whole emotional episode. But he felt he had to say, "I'm sorry."

"Don't be."

She turned back around to face him, revealing red-rimmed eyes. "No one has offered to help me with anything in this house. Even my friends. I don't know if they just don't feel like I would want them here, which I probably wouldn't. Or if they just don't want to be involved in such a morbid task. But I've done it all on my own."

She cleared her throat, then went on. "I can't tell you how much it means to me that you would offer, especially since you probably expected me to refuse."

"I had a feeling it might go that way."

"That's because you're a smart man."

Yeah...not. "I don't know about that, but I am persistent."

The laughter they shared broke the tension for a moment, but Blake wasn't about to let this go. "So you might as well tell me, what do you want to do with it?"

She swallowed. "I want to donate it. There's a nearby resident facility that assists elderly, end-of-life patients. I've wanted to donate it to them since my father died, but I have no way of moving it."

"I do believe I can handle that."

"*Then* maybe you can climb up on the roof for me," she teased.

"Only if there's an ambulance nearby."

It made Blake feel really good that he could help her smile through this task. He did his best clown impression while they packed everything up, and the two guys he called showed up with a truck to move it all. Madison only tensed up when they had to come into the house, but he was proud to say that she pushed through. She really wanted this to happen, and he felt sad that it had taken all this time for her to find a solution to this problem. That even though she had friends to help her, she didn't feel like she could call on them for that help.

The director of the facility knew her well, and was grateful beyond measure for her donation. They had a recently renovated room but hadn't managed to afford the furniture for it yet. Before he left, Blake slipped the director a check for a couple of thousand dollars to cover the rest of the furnishings. Now they could open the room for a new patient.

The fact that Madison thought to help someone during this time of grief humbled him beyond measure.

"You're my hero," she murmured against his lips as the truck pulled out of the driveway.

But Blake wasn't a hero. He was a wolf in sheep's clothing. She just didn't know it yet.

* * *

I love my husband so much. I would do anything for him, and even though I know his decision is stubborn and hurtful, I don't understand where he's coming from. He wants no part of my past. He wants to give no more power to a man who valued me only for my face and social graces. But I look at how much we need, how much we're hurting, and I know that selling that ring would make it all better. Why are men so stubborn?

Out of respect for him I've never mentioned this. Never so much as thought about it. Never wrote about my previous engagement in my journals and never talked about it with my daughter. I wish I could sometimes. Talk to her about the hard choices I made, how I knew my husband was the right one for me, how I chose love instead of money.

But I'd hate for her to know that my choice left our family ruined.

Madison reread the passage in confusion, burrowing down against the cushions of the chair in her bedroom. At first, it didn't even register what her mother was talking about. What previous engagement? But as she read through the passage once more, she realized the important part. Her mother had never spoken to her about this. Never spoken to anyone. The reason Madison couldn't find any hint of her previous life in these journals was because her mother chose not to talk about it out of respect for her husband.

Something had happened. Something that made

her mother have to choose, and while she knew that her father had been over the moon for his wife, that choice must have caused this traumatic thing that he'd never wanted to remember.

Selling her ring? What ring was she talking about? Madison couldn't remember her mother having any kind of ring except her wedding band set. It was the only thing of value that Madison had refused to sell. Despite how hard times became, she'd never sold them, even though it would've brought a modest amount. But it was her mother's wedding and tenth anniversary bands. Money could never replace that.

Had her mother kept a ring from a previous engagement? It had to be pretty substantial to be worth agonizing over the selling of it. Why had her mother not just given it back?

She scanned the entries right before that and found nothing relating to the ring. In the entry for the day before she mentioned it, she had lamented over the struggle to pay her husband's never-ending medical bills. Her father had recently been diagnosed with MS, she believed. At least the date looked close.

Then farther down in the entry for the same day, her mother wrote, *My husband says it will get better, but I fear the damage is permanent. He told me he would have his revenge, and he did. My husband's business will never be the same. My husband will never be the same. I hope the sacrifice was worth it for him, now and always. It would kill me to have my husband resent me in the end.*

So yeah, whatever happened was really bad. Madison felt a burning curiosity to know what it was. All this time her mother had written about daily life, the joys of motherhood, her love for her husband, and some of her deepest thoughts. But she'd never written or spoken of this matter and it was obviously a huge deal for her.

For them all.

Madison stood up and paced around her room. She wanted to talk about this, to tell someone. Her normal go-to would be her girlfriends. But Trinity's life was upside down enough already right now. She didn't need anyone butting in. And a glance at the clock told her that Tamika was still at work.

So who could she… How much would this kind of speculation annoy Blake?

She felt like they'd grown much closer, and his help the day before had touched her on a level that nothing else ever had. No one had ever helped her like that. Who else would see beyond a superficial need for food or companionship and go out of their way to help with something that she hadn't asked for? Frankly, she'd been floored.

Heck, he could have simply focused on the attraction between them and Madison would have been none the wiser.

But she'd done her best not to cry over him again, because he'd been obviously uncomfortable with her appreciation. She smiled. Her father had always been the same way. Tears made him panic. So she'd kept a stoic facade the entire time she'd known she was losing him.

Madison glanced back at the journal. But this was something fun, something mysterious. Something that intrigued her.

What could be the hurt in calling?

"Hey there," Blake said when he answered the phone.

The sound of that huskiness in his voice, so similar to the way he sounded when they were together, sent shivers down her spine. "Hey to you, too."

"What's up? You having a quiet day today?"

"Too quiet. I had to find ways to occupy myself, since you weren't coming over today."

"Well, if you're that desperate…"

She laughed at his teasing. "I got tired of sanding, so I've been reading my mother's journals, and you won't believe what I found out."

"Wait a minute. Your mother's *journals*?"

"Yes. She kept them for as long as I can remember. Although the oldest one I can find dates back to the first year of her and Dad's marriage."

The connection between them went oddly silent: no words and no breathing. Madison just figured it was a technical glitch and continued on.

"Anyway, today I was reading a passage from right after my dad got sick, and my mom talked about being engaged before."

Blake cleared his throat. "Engaged?"

"Yes! She said she was engaged and something terrible happened and my dad forbade her to ever talk about it."

"So that would mean…"

Again one of those weird silences, so she asked, "Are you there?"

"Hold on just a moment." She waited, until he finally said, "So do you think she left this guy for your dad? Do you know who he is?"

"She never says his name. She just says that she could sell the ring to help pay their medical bills, but my dad wanted nothing to do with it. Mysterious, right?"

Madison got excited just thinking about it. Who had the man been? What kind of ring was it? She started asking all these questions out loud to Blake, then realized after a few minutes that he hadn't responded. She paused.

"Blake?"

"Listen, Maddie, I need to go. Can I call you back in a little while?"

Disappointment had her dropping back into the chair in her bedroom. "Sure. Just whenever you're ready."

"I'll call you soon." *Click*.

Madison stared at her phone in consternation. That had been strange, and a tingling feeling of unease rippled through her once more. Even though Blake had said he wasn't keeping anything else to himself, she still felt like there were a lot of things about him that she had no clue about. Was this one of them? She didn't know what it could be… He could be conducting business. Seeing someone about his art. He never told her how that worked. But New

Orleans was filled with some very prestigious art galleries.

Was Abby okay? Madison bit her lip. It could have just been he was in a place that didn't have good reception. There was no sense worrying about this. And she knew she shouldn't, but that didn't stop her mind from running down the rabbit hole.

He would call her back. She just had to remember that.

Still, she was disappointed that he hadn't seemed too interested in what she found out about her mother. Maybe to other people it wasn't interesting, and Blake had never had strong familial connections. So it wasn't surprising.

But Madison had loved her mother to death, and been old enough to be really close to her before she passed away in a car accident. It was so unexpected, and Madison had grieved at night in private, but by day she had to continue on the work that she helped her mother with. She was still going to school, because her father had been functional enough that he could be left alone at that point. But the rest of her waking hours had been spent taking care of him or finding ways to financially support their family.

The ring sparked her curiosity. It seemed so tangible, this link to her mother's past. But she'd never seen one. Would her mother have hidden it? Gotten rid of it some other way? Sold it and just not told her dad where the money came from?

Madison's curiosity got the better of her, and she walked down the hall to her mother's room. Though her parents had shared a bed for a long time, the need for extra equipment and furniture for her dad, to accommodate his disability, had necessitated her mother moving her stuff into a separate room. In this big house there were plenty to choose from. They had gotten rid of a lot of things over the years after her mother passed away. That included most of her casual clothes, a few odds and ends other than those Madison had appropriated through the years, like her brush. All that had been left of her jewelry was costume pieces and her wedding set. Other than a few quilts her mother had made, the only things Madison had left were contained inside her mother's old chifforobe. She opened the doors, and was immediately met with the smell of lavender. It had been her mother's favorite scent. She'd often kept lavender sachets around the house.

Oddly, even after ten years, the scent still lingered on her clothes. Madison had chosen to keep some of her mother's more elaborate formal clothes. Dresses made from expensive materials. Her mother's favorite dressing gown—she would never call the beautiful piece of lace and satin a robe. A few pairs of heels that now fit Madison, but she'd never had occasion to wear them until recently. Madison searched through the clothes, though very few of them had pockets. Then she pressed against the back of the chifforobe, checking for any drawers or hidden compartments she might not have been aware of.

Finally she sat down in front of it and pulled out her mother's jewelry box. It was a gorgeous piece that her father had actually made, using beautiful cured maple and mother-of-pearl inlay. She could remember the Mother's Day he had given it to her. Madison was maybe ten or eleven? Her mother had been so happy. And genuinely shocked because he'd managed to keep the secret so well.

Her father had been a builder. He'd come from a modestly wealthy family himself, and he'd multiplied his fortune doing custom builds for the rich and famous of Louisiana. Madison had seen pictures of some of his houses, but he hadn't been able to keep it up and then he got sick. Losing his ability to work had eventually muted her father's love for life.

What had her mother meant about revenge and her husband's business? Madison had so many questions and so few answers.

But the beautiful box held nothing more than what Madison had seen over and over. A few costume pieces that her mother had let Madison try on through the years. But no true jewels. This used to surprise Madison, but now that she was an adult and knew just how much her father's illness had cost them, it didn't surprise her as much. She just assumed that whatever true jewels her mother's parents had given her had been sold through the years. Her mother had always been way more attached to people than things.

She set the jewelry box back into the bottom of the chifforobe and closed the doors.

As much as the mystery intrigued her, she would probably have to face the fact that her mother's secret had gone with her to her grave. Unless there was something later on in her journals. Madison thought she only had about six more months' worth to read.

She raced back down the hallway to pull the next journal from the box in her room. Money didn't matter. But her mother did. She might not find anything, but it was exciting to think the mystery could be solved.

Twelve

Blake watched nervously as the housekeeper settled the booster seat into the back of his car. Then she strapped Abigail in and turned to him.

"All ready," she said with a smile. "I know Abigail was looking forward to this. Thank you for taking her."

Blake just smiled and walked around to the passenger side. The smile masked a pool of unease in his gut. His father hadn't blinked when Blake had mentioned taking Abigail out with Madison. Instead he'd given simple consent.

Blake didn't trust that for one minute, but he couldn't divine any hidden motives and he didn't want to disappoint Abigail by going back on his word.

He hoped she would have a good time, because

he had absolutely no clue what he was doing. Which was why he'd broken down and asked Madison to help him. He felt guilty about terminating their call the day before, but he simply hadn't known what to say. He let her think that he had something else going on, because knowing that she'd been in the dark about her mother's previous engagement, and had no clue what kind of ring she was looking for, made him sick to his stomach.

He had no idea what to do and no idea what to say. Which was becoming a theme in his life right now. But he'd promised Abigail when he brought her home from the hospital that he would take her to do something fun. Why he had done that he wasn't sure, but he wasn't going to let her down. He refused to make her beg like her father did. He remembered what it was like to live the life that she had, where promises had been few and far between, and often broken.

He wasn't going to do that to her.

In the meantime, he hoped he could sidetrack any conversations about Madison's mother. His current plan was to just nod and say *uh-huh*. And offer absolutely no information whatsoever.

He could do that, right?

"Ready, kiddio?" he asked as he pulled out onto the highway.

He caught Abigail's nod in the rearview mirror, her grin infectious, her excitement palpable in the way she swung her little legs.

They stopped by to pick up Madison on their way

to City Park. "Are you excited, Abigail?" she asked
as she buckled herself in.

Abigail nodded enthusiastically.

"I think you'll have fun. There's lots of stuff to
do at City Park."

"But only until lunch," Blake cautioned. If it was
one complaint he'd heard about kids, it was that they
expected to do something forever. He didn't think
he was up to a marathon on his first outing with her.
Nor was she after her recent hospital stay…especially
in the summer heat.

Madison grinned at him, sharing a little secret.
"Definitely lunch."

Blake had to admit that City Park was an excel-
lent choice. Abigail especially liked Storyland Cas-
tle and the Puff the Magic Dragon slide. Madison
chased the little girl around the play area, so that her
giggles filled the air.

Then they headed back to see the frogs and birds
and turtles in the conservatory before strolling under
the live oaks with their hanging moss. Having met
her mother once after she had taken Abigail to a zoo,
Blake had known this would be a big hit. Abigail enjoyed watching the animals for a long time, and getting to take pictures of them with Blake's phone. The
only heartbreaking moment was when she asked,
"Can I send these pictures to my mommy?"

Madison turned away. Blake wished he had the
opportunity to do the same. "Absolutely, kiddio."

They didn't stop for lunch until Blake had taken
them on a bike ride and paddled Abigail around the

lake in a kayak. The whole time, Blake thought he
must be incredibly lucky. Abigail was laid-back and
easygoing, and he didn't have a single issue with
her. He did suspect that she was on her best behavior. He'd had more than enough of those moments
when he was a kid.

By the time they headed to lunch, he was feeling
much more comfortable. Maybe he didn't know how
to relate to Abigail as a child. But he related to her
the only way he knew how. He talked to her the same
way he would to anyone else. He didn't baby-talk her
or cater to her every whim. He simply urged her to
do things that looked fun, and when it was time to
move on to something else he was firm but polite.
It seemed to work well with this particular child.

They had lunch at a little kid-friendly café, where
Abigail got a grilled cheese and chips, eyeing the
cakes for later.

Madison talked about wanting to try one of the
recipes, and Abigail got all excited.

"Can I help? Sometimes Miss Sherry lets me help
her stir things. She says I do a good job."

Madison glanced his way before she said anything
and he gave a quick nod. He appreciated her checking in with him before offering anything, but how
could he say no to such a sweet little face?

Abigail was occupied talking about the different type of cakes she would like to make for quite
a while before she started to run out of steam. Her
eyelids got heavy, and she leaned against Madison
despite still having part of her sandwich left.

Blake sat in silence for quite a while, just enjoying the shade and the slight breeze in the courtyard.

Madison plucked a thread from the little girl's shirt as she finally said, "So I went through all of my mom's stuff yesterday."

Blake should've known it was coming, but still it was a stock. Even in his surprise he was able to murmur, "Yes?"

"I didn't find any kind of ring. Of course, I got rid of most of her stuff ten years ago. But you never know when there might be a hidden drawer, or a locked box somewhere."

Blake returned her smile, even though inside he felt slightly ill. It was only a few days ago that he himself had spent the night going through her entire house looking for just such a thing.

"I just wish I knew more about what happened. My mom's life at that time is such a blank for me. I think it would just be interesting to know."

And if she knew, she would be entitled to what she could find. But Blake had searched all over that house and found nothing. What the hell had happened to the Belarus diamond?

"For all I know, my mom could've sold an old engagement ring a long time ago. The only rings I could find were her wedding band set."

"So you kept them?"

Madison looked slightly surprised. "Of course. Granted, she could've sold them for a little bit of money. The diamond inside *was* worth something. But my mother was always more interested in people than things. She wouldn't have wanted to get rid of something my father gave her."

Abigail stirred slightly against her and Blake glanced down to see her lift sleepy eyelids. "Is she talking about Father's ring?"

Only years of having to hide himself from his father and present himself as someone he wasn't in society kept Blake's expression neutral. But inside, he was cursing up a storm.

Madison looked down at the little girl in question, but Blake quickly intervened. "No, sweetie. You just rest."

Who would've guessed that a seven-year-old listening from the top of the stairs could have absorbed so much? She was too smart for him to completely brush it off. Otherwise she would start asking more questions, he just knew it. "That was about something else, sweetheart."

Luckily, Madison kept right on, not really paying Abigail's question any mind. "I know it's a silly mystery, but I'm just curious."

Of course, she had no idea of the significance of what Abigail had asked. And her curiosity was something Blake couldn't relate to. After all, neither of his parents had ever been real people to him. Just evil dictators who should be avoided at all cost.

He'd thought that was all behind him, but look at him now.

Any minute, that very dictatorship was going to crush the most precious thing Blake had ever found in his life, if he didn't find a way to stop it.

Tonight he'd try to reach Abigail's mother one more time—and hope his luck held out for an alternative ending.

Madison took Abigail's hand in hers and led her away from the table with a smile at Blake. He'd really done well and handled way more things than she'd thought he would, but taking a little girl to the little girls' room might be asking a bit much.

The restrooms were in the far back of the little café. They paraded past the sandwich counter and the goody counter on their way. "I think I might have to ask Blake for one of those big Rice Krispies treats," Madison said. "Doesn't that look good?"

Abigail paused to look at the huge confection. "He won't want me to have that. My father says sweets rot your teeth."

Not an uncommon belief among older people. "Well, maybe if you only eat sweets and never brush your teeth. But you take good care of your teeth, right?"

"Sure do. See?" Abigail gave her an overly wide smile.

Madison dutifully inspected her teeth and pronounced them perfect. "I think we're safe to ask Blake anyway."

Abigail looked up at her, then asked, "Do you think my brother likes me?"

Madison glanced down with a frown. "Of course he does. Why wouldn't he?" She ruffled one pigtail. "After all, look how cute you are."

Abigail giggled but quickly sobered. "My father said that if I don't behave myself, Blake will leave and never come back. Just like my mommy."

Just the thought of anyone telling that to a small child took Madison's breath away. *Bastard.*

She led the little girl through the door to the restroom, and let it slide closed behind them. She knelt down next to Abigail. "Honey, I don't know what your father told you. But Blake is not going to leave if you misbehave. All children misbehave at some time or another. It's just a moment for them to have a learning experience."

Abigail's doe-brown eyes widened. "Really?"

"Really. It's just part of growing up. You'll get in trouble, but that doesn't mean that the people in your life don't still love you."

"Like you love Blake?"

No way was she going to admit that out loud to a child who might repeat it. "Blake is a very special man. And I think you'll find, if you give him a chance, that he will love you lots."

Abigail smiled, seeming satisfied, then went on to do her business. Madison knew her words were true. Blake might not have felt himself capable of it, but this last week had proved he had more than enough love to give. He'd just never known how to access it before.

Abigail took her time washing her hands, as she had plenty more questions for Madison. It seemed that her little nap had revived her energies quite well.

Some were as innocuous as, "Did you like the

tree frogs, too?" and "Can you bring me to the park again?" Then the uber serious, "Are you going to marry Blake?"

"Give it time, kid. Your brother and I haven't known each other that long."

Besides, the time they had been together had been quite tumultuous. Madison knew how she felt about him, but she was used to loss. Used to people leaving. And Blake had made no mention of emotions, though his actions spoke pretty loud. Still, she wasn't in any hurry to tell him her own feelings.

Abigail continued to chatter, which stopped the sweat from breaking out on Madison's brow. Hopefully she'd dodged a bullet there. She seemed to be handling the girl talk situation pretty well.

An unusually high number of the children who came through Maison de Jardin were boys. That was who Madison had the most experience with. She knew nothing about fixing hair or playing with dolls. A couple of teenage girls had come with their mothers to the shelter, but they weren't nearly as easy to befriend as the smaller kids.

"What is your mother's name?" Abigail asked.

Madison was a bit taken aback, and paused for a moment before answering. "It was Jacqueline."

"Was?"

Madison wasn't quite sure how much experience Abigail had with death, but she didn't believe in lying. "My mother died when I was younger."

"Were you a little girl like me?" Abigail asked,

standing at the sink while the water ran over her hands.

Madison wasn't sure how much she should tell a child this age. "She was in a car accident when I was sixteen."

"So she didn't leave you like my mommy?"

"No," Madison couldn't believe how horrible that must be for Abigail. She waited a moment before saying anything else to see what the little girl was thinking.

"My mommy left because I was too much trouble."

Damn. "Oh, Abigail, that's not true."

"Oh, it was. My mommy told me so a lot of times. I tried to be good, but I guess I wasn't good enough."

Pure rage swept over Maddie. How dare someone tell a child that. She was sure Abigail had been on her best behavior during this trip, but she still couldn't imagine a child being so bad that you would outright tell them you were going to leave because of them. She was sure many parents thought it during the course of a stressful day, but they would never say it out loud, because they honestly loved their children.

"I'm really sorry, Abigail."

"Father said Mommy is fragile." She tilted her head so she could look at Madison in the mirror. "What does fragile mean?"

Selfish was what Madison wanted to say, but instead she said, "It just means that someone might crack easily, like a glass."

"I knocked a glass off the table once and it shattered on the floor."

"Yes, that is fragile."

"Do you think I broke my mommy?"

Man, talking to kids was a minefield. "Absolutely not. That is not what I meant at all." She knelt down beside Abigail. "Your mommy being fragile has nothing to do with you. It has everything to do with your mommy. And I hope that she can find something while she's gone to make her stronger."

"You can become stronger?"

"Of course. You just have to exercise and eat your veggies." Madison pumped her arm to make a muscle, which caused Abigail to giggle.

Abigail finally finished with her handwashing, or what Madison would consider playing in the water, and got herself a couple of paper towels. As she dried off, she said, "I like you, but I do wish your ring had been Father's ring."

"How come?" Madison asked.

"It's what Blake needs. Father told him to get it."

"I don't think I understand," Madison said with a frown.

"I was listening on the stairs. Father didn't know, but I think Blake did. He and Father were arguing. Blake was mad because Father wouldn't take care of me."

She brushed her hands down over her little dress in an imitation of an adult. "Father said Blake could take me home with him, if he got the ring back. Otherwise Father would ignore me, or maybe send me away."

Madison could not wrap her mind around the horror of what she was hearing. Surely Abigail had to be mistaken.

"Your father told him to get the ring, from me?"

"I don't know." Abby scrunched her brows together. "That's what I thought he said. But he wasn't sure where it was."

"Maybe he was talking about someone else." *Please let him be talking about someone else.*

"Maybe so." Abigail looked up at Madison. "But I really want to go live with Blake. I can be really good and he won't want to send me away."

Since she wasn't sure what had been promised, Madison heard this hope with a touch of alarm. "Abigail, you realize Blake hasn't ever had children."

"I know." She shook her head vigorously. "But I can teach him how to have a little girl. I won't misbehave…much. Do you think he will help me learn?"

Madison blinked, desperate to not show tears in front of this girl who had been through so much in such a short amount of time. "I think you and Blake could teach each other a lot."

She gave Abigail a quick hug, then took her hand to lead her back to the table. Along the way, she had to wonder about the ring the little girl had mentioned. There was no way that could have anything to do with her.

But as she thought about those first days together, and her confusion over why Blake would want to be with her at all, the question wouldn't leave her. What ring had he and Armand been talking about?

Thirteen

"Quit blowing up my phone!"

For a moment Blake just looked at his cell phone, shocked. He'd called Abigail's mother, Marisa, over a dozen times, to no avail. Apparently she'd finally gotten tired enough of the noise to answer.

"Well, since I've run out of other options, I didn't know who else to call."

"Why are you calling me at all?"

Um, your child might need you?

That didn't seem to occur to her, as she went on, "The last thing I need to hear is how I have to come home. I am not coming home to that psychopath, and I can't find a new husband with a kid in tow."

Blake kept his mouth closed for just a moment. He wanted to lay into her about parental responsibility and how scared Abigail was and that she was really behaving like a child herself, but he couldn't. He had to help Abigail. He couldn't find the diamond. *Marisa* had to help him.

"Look, I'm just trying to figure out what's the best course of action. You left a very sick child in the hands of a man who couldn't care less about her."

"He doesn't need to care about her. That's what nannies are for."

Wow. How cavalier could she get? "He got rid of the nanny."

"Why?"

"You didn't see that coming? He let the nanny go. He said there was no reason to pay someone to watch out for her, because he doesn't believe that Abigail is really sick."

"Well, when he gets tired of dealing with her as much as I did, he'll get someone else. Doctor appointment after doctor appointment…"

"He's not going to take her to a doctor. He doesn't believe there's anything wrong. Your daughter is being neglected."

"She'll be fine," Marisa insisted. "He'll eventually hire a new nanny, and he'll take care of her. He's in a much better place to take care of her than I am. I'm broke."

"You just emptied your bank account. How can you be broke?"

Blake knew that wasn't the right question to ask. He just needed some answers.

"Look, I don't care. I don't care why you left. I

don't care that you're not coming back." Although he did care for Abigail, he just didn't want to get into that with Marisa now. "I just need to find out anything you can tell me so that I can take over Abigail's care."

"Don't bother. He's got more money than God. She's going to be much better off in his hands than her other options."

Blake had firsthand experience that said otherwise. The volcano of the emotions inside him erupted. "Really? An old man with a narcissistic personality disorder about to go broke is the best parent for a sick seven-year-old child?"

"What do you mean, *broke*?"

"Broke. No money. So if you think you're going to get a very nice settlement in the divorce, you can forget it."

Marisa was quiet for so long, Blake thought she might be reconsidering her actions. But no…

"I'm not supposed to get anything based on the prenup. Why do you think I'm out here trying to find somebody new? But Abigail is supposed to be taken care of."

There was no getting through to this woman. Blake insisted, "Well, there's nothing to take care of her with. He's basically housing her and that's it. She's already had one episode that landed her in the hospital."

"Well, if that's how it's going to be, she'd be better off with her real dad."

Blake held very, very still. It took him a minute to

absorb what she had just said. "Are you telling me… that Abigail is not his?"

"Well, she should be. I mean, we were married."

So? "Is she biologically his daughter?"

"Well, no."

Blake couldn't believe it. Of all the things he'd thought she might tell him, this was not one of them. He sat for a moment in stunned disbelief. He wasn't sure exactly how this would fix everything, but he knew it would. And he would make sure that it did.

"Why didn't you tell him?" he finally asked.

"I needed him to keep her. Besides, you know how he is. The minute he found out that I slept with somebody else, we'd both be out the door. He wouldn't put up for that kind of humiliation. And I'm too good to be a chauffeur's wife."

What should I do? What should I do? Blake racked his brain for an answer.

"Look, Marisa. Will you fill out paperwork that lets me take care of her?"

"Well, she's not gonna be in a good place with me. I just can't deal with that stuff. As a matter of fact, the first time I get the chance I'm closing this baby factory."

Nice. "But Abigail? Will you let me take care of her if I can find a way to make it happen? And before you ask, there's nothing in it for you. I'm all about Abigail right now."

"I guessed. Better double down over here if I'm gonna find a new man before Armand cuts me off. Take her."

Blake wanted to rail at the harshness of the conversation he just had as she clicked to disconnect. But he couldn't. He couldn't get lost over what Abigail did or did not have. He had to look to the future. He had to figure out how to use this new information to get what he needed. Without the diamond, this was his only option.

If he lost Maddie in the process, so be it. But at least she wouldn't have to know that he got involved with her under false pretenses. He didn't want to hurt her like that, even though walking away from her would leave him out in the cold for the rest of his life. He'd never found anyone like her before, and he doubted he ever would again. But he couldn't worry about that right now, or he'd be paralyzed with indecision.

Instead he needed to figure out what he had to do to take over parental rights. He had a feeling his father wouldn't want to be humiliated by having Abigail's true paternity made public. Not to mention his lack of funds for a lawyer to fight for custody once her mother handed her rights over to Blake.

He just had to hope in the end Abigail would have him. He wasn't that much of a catch as a father, but he'd at least try. Which was more than his own father had done.

Madison strode back and forth across her bedroom, the sound of the squeaking floorboards more than a little satisfying. She wasn't sure why; she wasn't accomplishing anything. And she wished she could. She wished that she could stomp her way right over to Blake's apartment and demand the truth. Even if her only source was a seven-year-old child.

She just wanted to know: Was Abigail right? Had Blake and Armand been talking about her? Had Blake honestly met and dated her to try to get something out of her? And if they wanted something from her mother, why had they waited all these years? She wanted answers, not more questions.

But she was also afraid to get those answers.

Madison paced furiously, anxiety sending her energy into hyperdrive.

Why had her mother told her none of this? She may have felt she owed her husband something, but what about her daughter? What about the life she left her to? And even though she knew her mom hadn't left willingly, she had chosen to delay the inevitable until it was too late, leaving Madison with an adult-size responsibility and very few resources.

How could she find the answers? She hadn't missed a journal. Out of desperation, she walked over to the box and glanced over the half dozen, leather-bound journals. As she ran her hand over the spines, she suddenly remembered the pieces of paper that had been stuck in her mother's journal the other day.

Shifting the books to the side, she found the papers in the bottom of the box where she'd dropped them before leaving last week. Excitement caused her to breathe hard as she unfolded them. There was more of her mother's handwriting on the pages, but this was different than the journal entries. This was addressed directly to her.

Dearest Madison,
I'm hoping you never have to read this. I'm hoping that the lawyer never has to give you this in the event of my death.

What lawyer? Had her mother planned to take this to the lawyer to go with her will, and never made it?

But I need to tell you a story. One that I should tell you in person, but I would do anything to not hurt your father. If I'm gone, you need to know this.

When I was young, before I knew my own mind, I went along with what my parents told me to do. That was the acceptable thing in that time, for girls of my class. That you obey your parents, learn how to talk and act, not be too smart, or too sassy. Marry well and be an asset to your spouse.

And I tried. I tried to make my parents happy. They were elderly, as I was a late-in-life baby, one that they never really expected to have. They always seemed frail in my mind and they didn't live very long past my marriage to your father. Anyway, when I was finally of marriageable age, I was pursued by a man named Armand Boudreaux. He was well known in our social circles, and his family was very wealthy. He was slightly older than me, and well on his way to making his own fortune.

Armand was mostly charming, but I quickly learned that he hid an often subtle cruelty. He wasn't in love with me but seemed to want to acquire me because I exceeded his qualifications for a wife. And I think, on some level, that he thought I would counterbalance what he knew he was lacking in himself: compassion and a genuine interest in other people. Which would help cement his social status.

At the same time, my parents were building a house, and I met a new young man. He was a very well-known architect and builder, rising quickly in fame and wealth. Handsome and articulate. I'll admit, I became obsessed. Your father was smart and charming, and he understood me in a way that neither my parents nor Armand ever had. He brought out the best in me, and didn't ridicule me for wanting to do things that didn't seem to fit with my social status. He taught me to refinish furniture, build things. He encouraged me to paint and take pictures—lots of things that my parents didn't understand.

It didn't take long before I was completely in love and stuck in a place I didn't know how to get out of. Though my parents loved me, they were quite old-fashioned. I'd made a promise to Armand, and they expected me to fulfill it. There was also the social pressure of know-

ing that their peers would be there to judge the decision that their daughter made, and thus it would reflect on them. Every generation has peer pressure; it just comes in different forms. But in the end I couldn't walk away from your father, so we eloped. On the eve of my wedding to Armand, I ran away with your father and left my parents and Armand letters telling them that I was sorry, but I could not go through with the wedding.

I had every intention of returning the ring. The engagement ring that Armand gave me was more than special. The diamond was a rare oval blue diamond called the Belarus diamond. Quite famous, and quite expensive. But upon my return, I found that Armand had embarked on his own form of revenge. I'd known he would be upset, and I suspected he would lash out. But I never anticipated what actually happened.

Armand went out of his way to ruin your father's business. The one time I approached him, he called me some quite inappropriate names, and honestly I was afraid of him, so I never approached him again. As time went on it became clear that your father might have to relocate to save his business, so I decided to hold onto the diamond as insurance for my family to hopefully save us from the ruination that I brought upon them.

Only we never had the chance to leave. Your

*father became ill and I thought the diamond
would be the only thing to save us. But your
father refused to allow me to sell it. He wanted
no part of Armand and refused to listen to me.*

*I could not go against his wishes, but I kept
the diamond and hid it, so that you, my daughter, would have it should you need it. It is yours
to do with as you wish. After all, it was a gift,
and it would be my wish that you should never
be so destitute that you feel like you cannot
sustain yourself or your loved ones. I know that
feeling well. And never ever want that for you.*

*I'm sorry that I couldn't make things easier.
I love you and your father more than I can ever
tell you. Be well, my child.*

Love, Jacqueline

Madison flipped to the next page to find di-
rections on where the diamond had been hidden.
She stared for a moment, uncomprehending, then
blinked. Her mother had put the diamond in a place
no one would ever have looked for it. *Genius.*

Without hesitation, she grabbed her shoes and ran
out the door. Her jog across the back trail to Maison de Jardin was familiar and yet felt longer than
she could have imagined. Her heart pumped from
the run and in anticipation of what she might find.
Would the diamond still be there?

The house was quiet during the day, with everyone gone to various jobs or school. Madison made

her way to the conservatory without running into anyone who might still be home, and quickly found the statue that her mother had indicated.

Madison stared at it. She had always seen the statue as a representation of this place's purpose. It was a little girl and her mother with their hands clasped and arms raised in dance. The purpose of this home had always been to bring happiness and joy to women and children who had been mistreated. To help them get back on their feet and find their dance again.

Finally Madison moved around to the back of the statue and started to dig at the mound of dirt around the base.

It took a couple of inches before she found the little compartment. Her smile felt like it lit up her whole body. Who knew there'd been a secret compartment all her life in the base of this statue?

Unfortunately she couldn't get it open, and had to go get a screwdriver to pry the edges apart. Finally it popped open, and Madison was able to work the little drawer out. Inside was a metal box, which she opened to find multiple layers of protective wrapping.

But as she pulled away layer after layer, Madison could not believe her eyes.

The fact that the diamond had an actual name should have been her first clue that it was something extraordinary. But that had kind of flown under Madison's radar. The oval-shaped jewel was a brilliant blue color, so brilliant it made her gasp. It shone against her dirt-stained fingers. The size would have made it very uncomfortable to wear, in her opinion, but she could see why someone like Armand would give it to his future wife. By doing so, he could prove he was the best husband in the world.

Only he didn't realize money wasn't everything.

Suddenly she understood what her mother meant. Selling this particular ring, this particular diamond, would have taken care of them for life, no matter how many medical bills her father had. Madison wouldn't have a house falling down around her ears. She wouldn't have had creditors banging on her front gate.

She wouldn't have had to spend her high school years working after school, or taking on other jobs while caring for her father.

Suddenly her elation faded. She could also now understand why someone might falsely portray himself, pretending to like or love her in order to get his hands on this.

Was Blake really capable of that? Was every moment they'd been together a lie? Madison had to know.

I know what you did. Meet me at ASTRA.

Blake clenched his fingers around his phone as he remembered the text he'd received from Madison last night. So he'd had an entire night to agonize over what had happened, wondering and worrying until he'd been sick to his stomach. She refused to answer her phone, which made him suspect she had turned it off after telling him when and where to be.

That wasn't like Madison at all, so he knew this was bad. Very bad. Which meant she'd found out something about the ring…and its connection to his family.

Had it been Abigail's innocent remarks over lunch that had alerted her? Had she found something in her mother's journals that made the connection with his family? Had she put two and two together and come up with the original plan his father had put into place?

Blake knew he couldn't change what had happened before, but if she'd found out part of the truth, would she listen to him when he told her what he was trying to do *now*? His true role in this entire mess? What he hoped worked—for both her sake and Abigail's?

He stepped into the rotunda to find her staring at a painting across from him, her arms wrapped tightly around herself. If he needed any evidence of her defensiveness, that would've been it. It wasn't a position he'd ever wanted to see her in again. It reminded him that too much had been thrown Madison's way. She deserved the best—much more than life had dished out to her.

He approached cautiously, giving her a chance to see him out of the corner of her eye before he reached her.

"Madison, what's going on?" he asked.

He expected tears or a defeated attitude. Instead

she seemed to almost closed down. Only her eyes seemed sad. "I know what happened. Abby told me."

"Abby told you what?"

Blake wished they weren't in the rotunda. All of a sudden he desperately needed something to lean on, to support his shaky legs, but even touching the walls in here would set off an alarm.

"When we went to the restroom, Abigail told me more about the ring. She recounted the conversation between you and your dad." She waved her hand in the air as if to erase her words. "In a roundabout kind of way. She didn't really know that it was about me. But it made me curious, so I went looking."

She reached into her purse and pulled out a box. A very expensive jewelry box. Blake held his breath as she opened it. Inside was the ring.

Of all the things Blake had expected to see today, that was not one of them. He stared for a moment, almost bemused. It was incredible, just like all the reports had said.

But he quickly moved his gaze back up to hers. There was no point in pretending anymore. "How did you find it?"

Madison sucked air into her lungs, blinking away tears at his implied admission. "My mother left me a letter. One that she never got a chance to give to the lawyer. I found it in one of her journals. She explained all about Armand. And quite frankly, after hearing that, I'm not surprised that she kept the ring."

"She was well within her rights to keep the ring," Blake insisted. "My father is…not an easy man."

"If he had just left them alone, she would've given it back."

"But he feels like he should have his cake and eat it, too. Which means being a major league asshole, and still getting his way."

Madison looked away, and he could see her bracing herself. She took a deep breath and straightened her back. "Why?" She glanced back at Blake and he could see the crack in the calm facade. The grief he'd never wanted her to experience again. She'd had enough loss. "Why would you do this? Why would you take it this far?"

He wished he could give an answer that left him looking squeaky clean. But he didn't have one of those tucked into his back pocket. "Maddie... Madison," he stumbled over the nickname after remembering her assertion that it should only be used by those who'd earned the privilege. "I just want you to understand that I never meant to hurt you."

"And you think finding out that you met me and dated me under false pretenses wouldn't hurt?" She stared at him for a moment. "Unless you never intended for me to find out?"

"There's really no way for me to defend myself against that," he said, utter defeat a physical weight on his chest. Because if he'd had his way, she would never have found out about any of this. He searched for a way to tell her the story that would not make him look like an insensitive jerk, but there really wasn't one.

"There's no point in me lying anymore," he conceded with a grimace. "I went into this knowing that I had to hide my motives from you. I thought it would be a date, maybe two, and then I'd be out of your life. It would all be over. No harm done, and no lasting repercussions for anyone but Abigail, who would have a better life. But that's not how it played out." He stared at her, aching to take away the hurt that bowed the lines of her body. "I knew with every move, every choice, that this wasn't right. But I simply could not stay away."

"And how I felt didn't play into it?"

"It did. But by that time I was in too deep and desperately searching for a way not to hurt you."

He didn't want to offer excuses, but she deserved more of an explanation. "It was obvious that you did not have the ring yourself and didn't know anything about it. I kept searching to keep my father at bay while I desperately tried to find some way to help Abigail."

"So what she said was true? Her father is going to…what? Trade his child for this?" She lifted the box once more.

He knew it was unbelievable. But having Armand as a father convinced Blake his father spoke the truth. "I told you he was a bastard. That's exactly what's happening. He wanted me to find the ring and get it back for him, and in exchange I will get full parental rights to Abigail."

She stepped closer as a couple of women walked into the rotunda and began discussing the paintings. "Why would a parent do that?"

"Madison, I've spent a lot of time with my father. And I've finally figured out that if you try to understand his motives, you're just going to spend a lot of time banging your head against a wall." He sighed. "No one can understand that, because we're not like him. He is his own selfish, narcissistic self. That's not going to change and the only option is to stop him at whatever cost. That's what I've been trying to do. Why I tried to keep him away from you before." But Blake feared he was fighting a losing battle. "Right now, I have to keep Abigail safe. Regardless of what I want, and regardless of the fact that I love you."

Madison's whole body jerked. Her eyes squeezed shut for a moment. "Please don't say things you can't mean."

Well, he hadn't meant to say it but… "I did mean it, Maddie, and I will always mean it. But I fully accept why that would mean nothing to you."

He reached out to grasp her arms in an effort to get her to look at him. The touch was bittersweet, as he knew it would be his last. "I'm more sorry than I can tell you. I didn't intend to get involved, I didn't intend to fall in love, and I had no idea what an incredible person you really are. But I have to save Abigail. I've lived that childhood, and I will not allow her to live it, too."

Madison nodded, though whether his words made sense to her, he wasn't sure. Then she explained. "I love you, too. But that's not why I am doing this. I'm doing it for Abigail, too, because no child deserves to live neglected and unloved. I've fought against that my entire life, and it's more important to me than anything."

She raised her hand between them. "That's why I want you to take this."

Blake blinked. He glanced down at the box, then back at her face. "I...don't...understand..."

"I want you to have this, so that Abigail will be taken care of."

Blake was already shaking his head. "Maddie, this was your mother's. It should take care of you for the rest of your life. Especially after you've given your life to take care of others."

She stared down at the box for a moment. "Taking care of others is not something that requires a reward. I did it out of love," she said, then pressed her lips together hard. As her eyelids drifted down, a single tear rolled over her cheek. "Just take it."

"I believe that belongs to me."

Heated fear washed over him as Blake turned to see his father walking across the rotunda, which was otherwise empty now.

"Thank you for finding it for me, Madison," Armand said. "That seems to be more than my son was capable of."

Madison began to extend her arm, and Blake quickly stepped in front of her to face his father. "Absolutely not. You are not taking this from her."

"But I thought you said Abby could live with you if I give this back?" Madison said.

"No, he said I can have her parental rights, if I *stole* this from you."

"I believe I have a claim," Armand insisted.

"It was a gift to Madison's mother. It doesn't belong to you anymore. If it did, your lawyer would have been able to get it back for you long ago."

Armand's practiced smile grew wider. "But I'm the one who would benefit most. Unless you count Abigail."

Madison gasped.

"I will fix this, Madison," Blake insisted.

His father studied him for a moment. For once, Blake felt no urge to shift in his shoes. This wasn't about meeting his father's expectations. This was about two different scales, and the fact that Blake was looking out for more than just himself.

"I never thought you would defend a woman," his father said.

Blake was a little taken aback. Why wouldn't he defend another person? He just didn't know a lot of people who needed defending. But then again, his father's measurements were based on his own warped standards, and Armand had never gone out of his way to defend anyone but himself.

"Some people grow up, Armand, and learn to deal with the consequences of their actions. That's what's happening here. As a consequence of my actions, I'm going to lose Madison. She's fully justified in walking away from me. And I'll let her because I betrayed her. You, on the other hand, have just lost your free ride."

"I have no idea what you're talking about."

"Madison doesn't need to give you that diamond.

It will have no effect on Abigail. Because you have no claim to her."

"That doesn't even make sense. I'm her father."

"You *thought* you were her father, biologically at least. But you're not. She's not even yours. I can get a DNA test to prove this and have her taken away. Or you can sign over your rights."

He should've been satisfied that his father looked stunned, but it didn't make him feel good to take the old man down. It only felt good to know that Abigail would be safe. "If you sign over your rights, I'll pay you enough to get back on your feet, and you can dissolve your marriage with no contest." He straightened, hoping his height advantage would convince his father he wasn't to be messed with.

"If you refuse, I'll make sure everyone in your social circle knows that your wife cheated on you with the chauffeur. That you've raised a child who wasn't yours all these years, and blackmailed your son into stealing from another woman for your benefit."

Behind him Madison gasped, but Blake couldn't stop now. "I have nothing to lose," he said. And that was true. Without Madison, he would never be truly happy again. "You do. So are you going to take the easy way out, or lose your reputation along with your fortune?"

Only someone who'd lived with Armand all these years would know just how much his reputation meant to him. Not to mention the fact that it was his only way of getting his business back on its feet.

His connections within Louisiana society, and the country as a whole, were his only source of revenue.

"Do you really expect me to give up a fortune to the daughter of my enemy?" he asked, his genteel facade slipping even further with his sneer.

"He wasn't your enemy," Madison said from behind him. "He was just a man who actually loved my mother. Not one who wanted her to enhance his reputation and social status."

"And that, Father, is the problem with your life in a nutshell. You just want to keep up appearances. Not to mention the fact, if you walk away now, Madison won't have to take out a restraining order against you."

For a moment, Blake thought his father might burst an artery. His entire face flushed and he practically shook with anger.

"So what will it be, Father?" Blake prodded. "Should I contact your lawyer?"

Armand visibly pulled himself together. "Of course," he said in a clipped, controlled tone. No yelling would be allowed in public today, Blake guessed. Then Armand turned on his heel and walked away, ever displaying the calm veneer of a wealthy gentleman, hiding the snake lurking beneath.

"How much is that going to cost you?" Madison whispered.

"It doesn't matter. As long as I can support Abigail, we'll be good." He turned back to face her. "I'm so sorry, Madison. You didn't deserve that. Any of it."

Reaching out, he wrapped her fingers around the

jewelry box. "Take this to Trinity, and ask her to find you someone reputable to sell it." He swallowed hard. "I need to know that you're taken care of in the way you deserve."

Madison stared down at the box for several moments before she glanced back up with tears in her eyes. "What makes you think I deserve the money from this?"

"Life. You've had a raw deal, Madison. You deserve far more than life has given you."

"And yours wasn't just as bad? At least my parents loved me. I didn't have to live under that guy's thumb my entire life. That was a close call, I'd say."

Blake cocked his head to the side. Was she actually joking? "Um, yes. I'd agree."

"Blake." She drew in a deep, hard breath. "I believe I've come to a decision."

This is it. Here comes the goodbye.

She held up the jewelry box, staring at it. "I believe that I'm going to need help taking care of this incredible piece."

"Yes?"

"I think you and Abigail would be perfect for the job."

What? "I don't understand."

"Well, I can't ask just anyone. I need someone who really knows me, knows what I believe in. It has to be someone I can trust."

"That would not be me." *It couldn't be me.*

"Are you sure?"

Blake swore as he broke out in a cold sweat. "What are you saying?"

"Yes, you lied to me. You met me under false pretenses and kept secrets from me."

"Yes, I did, Madison. I'm sorry."

"And I know you really are. Do you know how I know that?"

Blake shook his head, not trusting his voice.

"Because you just volunteered to give up a fortune to take care of a child who isn't even yours."

Her dark green gaze made his head swim. Was she really saying this?

"I know better than to think that your father will let you off cheap. And I know better than to think that raising a young girl alone doesn't scare the pants off you." She stepped in closer, bringing her heat to mix with his. "Those are the things that are important to me. That's the Blake I fell in love with—the man who isn't perfect but is trying his best..." She brushed her lips over his, pulling a heartfelt sigh from him. "And his best feels pretty darn good."

Blake struggled to keep his wits about him. "How do you know I wasn't lying? That I'm not lying now?" Maybe he was a fool to ask, but he'd rather know for sure before he fell too deep to dig himself out.

"It's quite simple, really," she said. "All I need is your response to my plan."

"You have a plan?"

"I do. And only the best of men would go along with it."

Blake wouldn't consider himself the best of men, but somehow he knew he'd support Madison in anything she wanted to do. He couldn't hold back. He wrapped his arms tightly around her and buried his face in her neck. "I love you, Madison."

"I love you, too," she whispered.

Then he pulled back. "You know we come as a package deal now—Abby and me?"

"Absolutely…" She waited for a moment, then asked, "So, don't you want to know the plan?"

"It doesn't matter. I got the girl…girls. That's all I need."

Epilogue

Madison watched as Abigail charmed an older couple who had come to the exhibit. This might be the little girl's "debut," but without a doubt, in her frilly dress and hair ribbons and curls, she was stealing the show from the main attraction.

Blake stood at the entrance to the rotunda at the ASTRA, ready to answer any questions people might have. In the past year, he'd become an expert on the Belarus diamond and its caretaker of sorts. Madison couldn't believe that he'd gone along with her plan. But he'd not only supported her, he'd embraced the purpose behind it and spent every day helping her fulfill her goal.

To use the Belarus diamond to create funding for those in need.

To that end, they'd arranged with the museum to exhibit it here for special functions. Part of the ticket proceeds would go to fund Maison de Jardin and charities like it. Ownership had been officially established with the charity. Madison didn't need or want the jewel. She had all she needed with her fiancé and the half sister who was now legally his child.

Trinity stepped up to her, resting her arm around Madison's shoulders as she took a sip of her sparkling water. No champagne for the mom-to-be.

Trinity's happy-ever-after had come around the same time as Madison's. The chaos and suspicions surrounding her first marriage and husband's death had been tough, but she'd been rewarded with a new husband...and a family of her own. Michael Hyatt's estates were in good hands, Trinity's hands, and Maison de Jardin was protected from vultures like Michael's relatives.

But even more important, the business consultant they'd hired was now Trinity's new husband. He'd rocked the Secrets and Scandals blog with his revelations, and come out on the other side as Trinity's biggest supporter and the father of her unborn baby. Their story was still a source of extreme interest from New Orleans' society.

"How's the second attraction of this little charity exhibit doing?" Madison asked with a chuckle.

Trinity grimaced. "Who knew so many nosy people would want to stare at a pregnant lady?"

"Only if said pregnant lady was the most talked about heiress in all of Louisiana..."

Trinity arched a brow in her direction. "You haven't done so bad yourself. I thought the phone would never stop ringing once your story broke."

"We both ended up with some pretty spectacular legacies, didn't we?"

Trinity smiled. "Funny how they weren't as important as the people that came with them, huh?"

Even if they weren't still here. They'd dedicated tonight's event to Madison's parents and Trinity's late husband, Michael, who had helped found Maison de Jardin.

But those legacies had brought other people into their lives: for Trinity, her new husband and the baby she was expecting, and for Madison, Blake and Abigail. For the first time in a long time, Madison's life felt full. Full to overflowing.

Blake's gaze caught hers from across the room. The intensity of his feelings reached her even though they weren't speaking. Not a day went by with him that wasn't her best. But tonight...tonight was special.

Somehow they both knew it.

Tamika sidled up to the girls, smiling over her champagne flute. "Ladies, I'm getting lucky tonight."

Madison and Trinity exchanged a glance. Tamika ignored them. "I figure all of this good luck has to rub off sometime. Trinity is married. Madison is getting close. We think. Surely it's my turn next."

"Go stand next to Blake."

"Why?"

"He's the lucky one."

"I didn't need to know that," Tamika said with a laugh.

"No, really. Today's the day."

Tamika and Trinity leaned in close. Madison smiled, unable to resist letting them in on the secret. She wiggled her fingers. "Because tonight, I think I'll let him put a ring on it."

* * * * *

Scandal and seduction
go hand in hand
in the
Louisiana Legacies
duet:

Entangled with the Heiress
Reclaiming His Legacy
by Dani Wade

Available exclusively
from Harlequin Desire!

WE HOPE YOU ENJOYED
THIS BOOK FROM
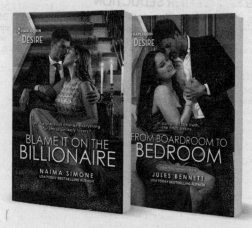

*Luxury, scandal, desire—welcome to
the lives of the American elite.*

Be transported to the worlds of oil barons, family dynasties,
moguls and celebrities. Get ready for juicy plot twists,
delicious sensuality and intriguing scandal.

6 NEW BOOKS AVAILABLE EVERY MONTH!

COMING NEXT MONTH FROM

⟨H⟩ HARLEQUIN
DESIRE

Available March 3, 2020

#2719 SECRET HEIR SEDUCTION
Texas Cattleman's Club: Inheritance • by Reese Ryan
Fashion mogul Darius Taylor-Pratt is shocked to learn he's the secret heir of
the wealthy Blackwood family! That's not the only surprise as he reconnects
with his ex, diamond heiress Audra Lee Covington. As old passions flare, new
revelations threaten everything...

#2720 HEARTBREAKER
Dynasties: Mesa Falls • by Joanne Rock
Gage Striker vows to protect Mesa Falls Ranch from prying paparazzi at
any cost—even when the press includes his former lover, Elena Rollins. Past
misunderstandings fuel current tempers, but will this fire between them reignite
their attraction?

#2721 JET SET CONFESSIONS
by Maureen Child
Fiona Jordan is a professional fixer and her latest job is bringing billionaire
Luke Barrett back to his family business. As she goes undercover, the sparks
between them are instant and undeniable. But she learns not everything is easy
to fix when Luke discovers her true identity...

#2722 RECLAIMING HIS LEGACY
Louisiana Legacies • by Dani Wade
Playboy Blake Boudreaux will do anything to protect his family...including
seducing the beautiful philanthropist Madison Armantine to get back a beloved
heirloom. But as the secrets—and desire—between them grow, he'll have to
reveal the truth or lose her forever...

#2723 ONE NIGHT WITH HIS RIVAL
About That Night... • by Robyn Grady
After a night of passion, smooth-talking cowboy Ajax Rawson and successful
life coach Veda Darnel don't expect it to happen again...until it does. But will
old family business rivalries threaten to end their star-crossed romance before
it even begins?

#2724 THE DATING DARE
Gambling Men • by Barbara Dunlop
Jilted by their former lovers, friends James Gillen and Natasha Remington vow
to reinvent themselves and maybe find love again in the process. But their
daring new makeovers reveal a white-hot attraction neither was expecting...

**YOU CAN FIND MORE INFORMATION ON UPCOMING HARLEQUIN TITLES,
FREE EXCERPTS AND MORE AT HARLEQUIN.COM.**

HDCNM0220

*When billionaire bad boy Mercury Steele discovers his
car is stolen, he's even more shocked to find out who's
in the driver's seat—the mysterious beauty
Sloan Donahue. As desire and secrets build between
them, has this Steele man finally met his match?*

Read on for a sneak peek at
Seduced by a Steele
by New York Times *bestselling author Brenda Jackson.*

"So, as you can see, my father will stop at nothing to get what he
wants. He doesn't care who he hurts or maligns in the process. I
refuse to let your family become involved."

A frown settled on his face. "That's not your decision to make."

"What do you mean it's not my decision to make?"

"The Steeles can take care of ourselves."

"But you don't know my father."

"Wrong. Your father doesn't know us."

Mercury wondered if anyone had ever told Sloan how cute
she looked when she became angry. How her brows slashed
together over her forehead and how the pupils of her eyes became
a turbulent dark gray. Then there was the way her chin lifted and
her lips formed into a decadent pout. Observing her lips made him
remember their taste and how the memory had kept him up most
of the night.

"I don't need you to take care of me."

Her words were snapped out in a vicious tone. He drew in a
deep breath. He didn't need this. Especially from her and definitely
not this morning. He'd forgotten to cancel his date last night with

Raquel and she had called first thing this morning letting him know she hadn't appreciated it. It had put him in a bad mood, but, unfortunately, Raquel was the least of his worries.

"You don't?" he asked, trying to maintain a calm voice when more than anything he wanted to snap back. "Was it not my stolen car you were driving?"

"Yes, but—"

"Were you not with me when you discovered you were being evicted?" he quickly asked, determined not to let her get a word in, other than the one he wanted to hear.

"Yes, but—"

"Did I not take you to my parents' home? Did you not spend the night there?"

Her frown deepened. "Has anyone ever told you how rude you are? You're cutting me off deliberately, Mercury."

"Just answer, please."

She didn't say anything and then she lifted her chin a little higher, letting him know just how upset she was when she said, "Yes, but that doesn't give you the right to think you can control me."

Control her? Was that what she thought? Was that what her rotten attitude was about? Well, she could certainly wipe that notion from her mind. He bedded women, not controlled them.

"Let me assure you, Sloan Donahue, controlling you is the last thing I want to do to you." There was no need to tell her that what he wouldn't mind doing was kissing some sense into her again.

Don't miss what happens next in
Seduced by a Steele
by Brenda Jackson, part of her Forged of Steele series!

Available April 2020 wherever
Harlequin Desire books and ebooks are sold.

Harlequin.com

HDEXP0320